Jenny stared at him, at his sexy dark eyes and his silver-kissed black hair, at his powerful broad shoulders.

At all that *manliness*.

All that manliness that was here, in her house, all the time now.

She didn't need all that manliness sitting at her table every night, tempting her to forget who she was, who *he* was, who they were to each other. Tempting her to indulge herself in certain…feelings. Certain dangerous, impossible, terribly disturbing feelings that could never go anywhere….

Jenny pulled her raging thoughts up short. What was the matter with her? After all these years, had she suddenly developed a thoroughly embarrassing *crush* on Nick?

Dear Reader,

Hold on to your hats, because this month Special Edition has a lineup of romances that you won't soon forget!

We start off with an extraordinary story by #1 *New York Times* bestselling author Nora Roberts. *The Perfect Neighbor* is the eleventh installment of her popular THE MACGREGORS series and spotlights a brooding loner who becomes captivated by his vivacious neighbor.

And the fun is just beginning! *Dream Bride* by Susan Mallery launches her enchanting duet, BRIDES OF BRADLEY HOUSE, about a family legend which has two sisters dreaming about the men they are destined to marry. The first book in the series is also this month's THAT SPECIAL WOMAN! title. Look for the second story, *Dream Groom,* this May.

Next, Christine Rimmer returns with a tale about a single mom who develops a dangerous attraction to a former heartbreaker in *Husband in Training.*

Also don't miss the continuing saga of Sherryl Woods's popular AND BABY MAKES THREE: THE NEXT GENERATION. The latest book in the series, *The Cowboy and his Wayward Bride,* features a hardheaded rancher who will do just about anything to claim the feisty mother of his infant daughter! And Arlene James has written a stirring love story about a sweet young virgin who has every intention of tempting the ornery, much-older rancher down the wedding aisle in *Marrying an Older Man.*

Finally this month, *A Hero at Heart* by Ann Howard White features an emotional reunion romance between an honorable hero and the gentle beauty he's returned for.

I hope you enjoy this book, and each and every novel to come!

Sincerely,

Karen Taylor Richman
Senior Editor

Please address questions and book requests to:
Silhouette Reader Service
U.S.: 3010 Walden Ave., P.O. Box 1325, Buffalo, NY 14269
Canadian: P.O. Box 609, Fort Erie, Ont. L2A 5X3

CHRISTINE RIMMER
HUSBAND IN TRAINING

Silhouette ®

SPECIAL ✦ EDITION ®

Published by Silhouette Books
America's Publisher of Contemporary Romance

For the real Daisy…

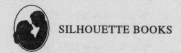 SILHOUETTE BOOKS

ISBN 0-373-24233-6

HUSBAND IN TRAINING

This edition published by arrangement with Harlequin Books S.A.

® and TM are trademarks of Harlequin Books S.A., used under license.
Trademarks indicated with ® are registered in the United States Patent
and Trademark Office, the Canadian Trade Marks Office and in other
countries.

Printed in U.S.A.

Books by Christine Rimmer

CHRISTINE RIMMER

came to her profession the long way around. Before settling down to write about the magic of romance, she'd been an actress, a salesclerk, a janitor, a model, a phone sales representative, a teacher, a waitress, a playwright and an office manager. Now that she's finally found work that suits her perfectly, she insists she never had a problem keeping a job—she was merely gaining "life experience" for her future as a novelist. Those who know her best withhold comment when she makes such claims; they are grateful that she's at last found steady work. Christine is grateful, too—not only for the joy she finds in writing, but for what waits when the day's work is through: a man she loves who loves her right back, and the privilege of watching their children grow and change day to day. She lives with her family in Oklahoma.

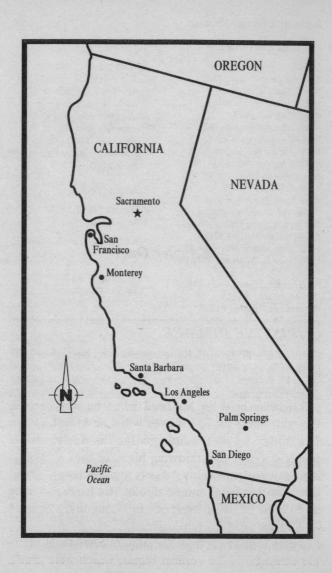

Chapter One

In the middle of a cold Saturday night in late February, Jenny Brown sat on the couch in her family room, sipping a glass of Chenin Blanc, thumbing through the photo albums she usually never allowed herself to look at, trying to remember…

Everything.

The way he'd tilt his head when he was deep in thought. The light in his eyes when he looked at her. His smile: so sweet, a little goofy. The way he would laugh at a joke, just throwing his head back and braying out his pleasure, his Adam's apple bobbing up and down on his long, tanned throat. His hands, so long and slender. Like the rest of him. Long and slender.

And the smell of him. Like…

Jenny looked up from the album. She stared off in the direction of the vertical blinds, which were drawn shut now, over the glass door that led out to the back-yard. She closed her eyes, breathed in through her nose.

The smell of him. Like…

But nothing came. She couldn't remember. Couldn't call up that special, particular scent that had been his alone. Oh, she could put words to it. It had been some-what sharp, in a clean way. Like a fresh-cut Christmas tree, when you bring it in that first day, and stand it up in the house. Yes, clean and sharp as the smell of pine. And a little bit sweet, like honey and sunshine all mixed up together.

But those were just words. Words Jenny remem-bered, from all the times before, when she had called up the scent of him and it had come to her, stunning and hurtful and achingly real.

Now, it wouldn't come. Only words would come.

The years had done what years do: they had stolen the scent of him away from her.

Jenny slowly brought the wine to her lips. She took a sip, swallowed, set the glass on the oak coffee table in front of her, to the left of the stack of photo albums. She looked down at the open album in her lap. At Andrew and her younger self, arms around each other, standing under a basketball hoop over at Oki Park.

Grinning. Both of them grinning. Neither of them knowing what a hideous surprise life had in store.

She touched his face, in the photograph. ''Oh, An-drew—''

As she said his name, the front doorbell chimed.

Jenny stiffened. Who in the world…? It was so late. She glanced at her watch. Past two.

Carefully she closed the album and set it on top of

the stack on the coffee table. Then she stood, went up the two steps to the dining area and through the open doorway to her small kitchen. From there, she could peek through the blinds that covered the window over the sink and see who had decided to ring her doorbell so late at night.

It was Nick DeSalvo, Andrew's best friend since both of them were little boys, standing there with his big shoulders hunched against the cold and his hands stuffed in his pockets. He was looking down. But he must have heard the blinds rattle against the window, because his dark head came up and he saw her. "Can I come in?" He more mouthed the words than said them.

She dropped the blind and hurried out of the kitchen, back through the dining area and into the small foyer next to the formal living room that she rarely used. She fiddled with the chain and dead bolt, then pulled the door open.

"Nick. What is it? Are you all right?"

He didn't answer. He appeared to be studying the toes of the expensive-looking boots he wore.

Jenny wrapped her arms around herself, shivering a little in her thin leggings and stocking feet. "Nick?"

At last, he spoke. "Sasha left me," he said to his boots. "She told me last week that she loved me. Yesterday, we had a big fight. And then today, when I got home, I found this...." He looked up then, dark eyes beneath heavy black brows brooding and uncharacteristically somber. "Here. Have a look." He stuck out a rumpled square of paper.

Jenny took the paper. By the porch light she read, "It's over, Nick. Don't try to contact me again. Goodbye.'' She handed the note back to him. ''What? What's over?''

Nick sighed heavily and shook his head. ''It was on my pillow. She left it on my pillow, along with the key I gave her, so she could get in the house anytime she wanted to.'' He tucked the note into a pocket.

Jenny wrapped her arms around herself again and watched her own breath plume in the icy air, waiting for him to say more. But Nick only stared at her, mute appeal in his eyes. ''Nick. Why don't you come on in?''

He smiled then—that real guy's guy smile of his, the one that drove all the women crazy. ''Hey. I thought you'd never ask.''

Jenny reached out, took hold of his big, muscular arm and pulled him over the threshold. He started right for the family room as she took a minute to lock things up again.

He was already parked on one end of the couch when she caught up with him short seconds later. She hovered a few feet away, mindful to take care of her hostess duties before she herself sat down. ''Come on. Take off your coat.''

He shrugged out of it, rose to his feet for a moment and gave it a toss. It landed on the armchair in the corner, by the TV. Nick dropped back to the couch.

''Do you want a drink or something?''

Nick skimmed both blunt-fingered hands back over the crown of his head. The gesture didn't do a thing to his hair. It was thick and black, shot prematurely with glints of silver. He always kept it short enough that neither a comb nor his own raking hands could have much effect on it.

She offered again, "Hey. A drink. Yes or no?"

He seemed to shake himself. "Uh-uh. I tried that. It didn't help."

Jenny went ahead and dropped to the other end of the couch. "Okay, then talk to me. Tell me all about this woman named Sasha."

He glanced around, frowning. "Polly's in bed, huh?"

Jenny gathered her legs up to the side and pulled the hem of her huge sweatshirt over her knees. "Nick. It's two in the morning."

For a moment, he looked disappointed; he adored Jenny's thirteen-year-old daughter. But then he shrugged. "Right. Two a.m. A kid should be in bed at two a.m."

"Exactly."

"Hell, Jen. I know I shouldn't have bothered you. But after I went out and tried to get drunk, I realized I needed a friend to talk to."

"It's okay."

"Besides, if I didn't come here, I'd have to go home. And you know what?"

"What?"

"I realized something else tonight. I hate my house."

Jenny made a sympathetic sound. Nick's house was new and big and expensive. He'd had it built by his own construction company and he'd hired a big-name interior decorator to furnish it for him. Thus, it was an interior decorator's idea of where a successful bachelor ought to live, a testament to the rags-to-riches success of Nick DeSalvo, general contractor turned real estate developer. Five thousand square feet of steel and glass and pricey modular furniture. In Jenny's opinion, a person would find more comfort on a slab at the morgue.

A slab at the morgue.

A grim analogy, but fitting, considering the date.

Nick's dark gaze made a pass over her, taking in her leggings and faded CSUS sweatshirt. "Hey. You weren't in bed, were you?" He glanced around a little, spotted the stack of photo albums on the coffee table, next to the nearly empty glass of wine. He understood then. "Andy, huh?"

Jenny forced a wobbly smile. "Four years to the day—as of five hours from now."

February 23, early in the morning. Because of those jelly doughnuts he loved. He'd gotten up at 6:50 and told Jenny to get the coffee on. He wanted jelly doughnuts and he was running over to the doughnut shop on Folsom to pick up a half dozen. He would share them with Polly, since jelly-filled were her favorite kind, too. But what kind did Jenny want?

Jenny had yawned and stretched, then murmured, "Chocolate-covered old-fashioned."

He bent over her. One last kiss. "Chocolate-covered old-fashioned, it is." And he was gone.

Forever.

Down the couch, Nick held out his big arms. "C'mere." With a little self-pitying sigh, Jenny slid over to him. He enfolded her in a hug. It felt good, to rest against him, to hear the strong, steady beat of a friend's heart.

"I was thinking about him tonight, too," Nick whispered against her hair.

She snuggled a little closer, indulging herself. Nick

had such strong arms, such a broad, deep chest. She always felt safe whenever he hugged her. "Really?"

"Uh-huh. I still miss him." He rubbed her gently on the back. "And I shouldn't have showed up here. I should have left you alone."

"That's not true." She gave up the comfort of his arms, straightening from his embrace and resolutely retreating to her own side of the sofa. "What's a friend for, if you can't come knocking on her door when you need her? And besides, I think I was getting kind of maudlin, sitting here all alone, looking at old pictures, feeling sorry for myself." She made a little show of getting comfortable all over again, drawing up her legs and tugging her sweatshirt hem over her knees. "Okay. Let's talk about you."

"Jenny—"

"No." His hand lay along the sofa back, very near her own. She gave it a motherly pat. "I mean it. Tell me about this Sasha person."

Those thick brows got a little closer together as he frowned in obvious puzzlement. "Didn't you meet her? I thought you met her."

"I don't think so. How long have you known her?"

"Three weeks."

"Uh-uh. We haven't seen you since about a month ago."

"Come on. It can't have been that long."

"Yes, it has. It was the end of January. Remember, you took Polly to that basketball game in San Francisco?"

"Oh. Right." He grunted. "The Bulls played the Warriors. The *Bulls*. Michael Jordan. Scottie Pippen. I mean, these are the giants of the game. And how many more years have they got, do you think? Any kid who gets a chance to see them in the flesh is one lucky kid. But Polly, she just kept *yawning* through the whole damn game. Andy's kid. And she yawned through a Bulls game.''

Gently Jenny reminded him, ''Polly has…other interests.''

''Yeah, right. Emily Dickerson, I heard all about her.''

''It's *Dickinson*. Emily Dickinson.''

''Whatever.''

''And, as I said, we never got a chance to meet this Sasha.''

He let out a long, heartfelt sigh. ''Well. Sasha was perfect.''

There was still a little wine left in Jenny's glass. She picked it up and finished it off. ''Perfect for what?'' She set her glass back on the coffee table.

''For me. For my wife.''

Jenny's mouth dropped open in pure amazement. ''Your *wife?* Since when do *you* want a wife?''

Nick shifted on the couch, facing front now, planting his booted feet apart, hunching over and resting his arms on his thighs. ''Since…lately. Since I've been thinking that something is missing.'' He shot her a sideways glance. ''And you don't have to look at me like that.''

''Well, but, Nick…''

'''But, Nick' what?'' His strong, square jaw had jutted out even farther, in pure defensiveness.

''Well, I mean…''

''*What?*''

She still didn't answer. She was too busy recalling

a few remarks Nick had made over the years in regard to women and matrimony. Things like, "Why buy a cow when there's so much cream around?" and "If I wanted to be tied down, I'd hire one of those sweeties in black leather with a whip."

"I want to get married, damn it." Now Nick sounded downright defiant. He was sitting up straight and glowering at her.

She put up both hands. "Okay, okay. So you want to get married. To Sasha…"

"Overfield. Sasha Overfield."

"Why to Sasha Overfield?"

"Because Sasha's the woman I've been waiting for all my life." He slumped back on the couch and stared morosely down at his spread knees. "I went to the damn *opera* with her, Jenny. That's how serious I was."

"Wow. I am impressed."

He turned to look at her. "I may be a lunkhead, but I know sarcasm when I hear it."

"Wait a minute. Did I call you a lunkhead?"

"No, *you* were sarcastic. Sasha's the one who called me a lunkhead—a lunkhead in a hard hat is how she put it."

"But why would she call you a lunkhead? Didn't you say that *she* said she loved you?"

"She did. And 'lunkhead' is not a word a woman like Sasha would normally use. But she was frustrated. Because she doesn't *want* to love me."

"Why not?"

"Because she wants to get married."

"That's a problem? You just said *you* want to get married."

"Right. We both want to get married. But she thinks I'd make a lousy husband. She says I'm insensitive. That I would never be *there* for her in the tough times, since I'm not in touch with my inner child *or* my feminine self. That I have no *romance* in my soul. She also said that we have no common interests, so as soon as the hot sex wears off, we'll end up in the divorce courts."

Jenny rejected the idea of exploring the issue of hot sex. She asked, briskly, "Aside from the opera, what *are* Sasha's interests?"

"Huh?"

"Her interests, Nick. What are her favorite things? What activities does she enjoy?"

"Well." He slumped deeper into the couch cushions as he pondered the question. Finally he said, "She's got a cat. A really fat one that she's crazy about. And her apartment is full of books. She's a *reader,* you know?" He glanced across the room at the two big, full bookcases that flanked the sliding glass door. "She's like you and Polly that way. Also, she's big on art and nutcases."

Jenny resolutely did not roll her eyes. "Art and *nutcases?*"

"She's studying to be what they call an art therapist. An art therapist has people look at paintings and draw things to work out their problems."

This is a match made in hell, Jenny thought. Right up there with Eleanora Mandeath, the feminist performance artist he'd dated for about a month. And Betsy Faith, the manic-depressive flugel player from some coal mining town in England. Nick and Betsy had been an item for about three weeks.

"How, exactly, did you meet Sasha?"

He glanced away, muttered, "The Nine-Seventeen Club," and then looked back at her, as if daring her to disapprove of the fact that he'd met his true love at one of Sacramento's most popular singles' bars, the kind of place where, if one did find *true love,* it rarely lasted longer than one night.

Nick shook his head. "I know, I know. That place is a meat market. But Sasha was lonely. And I was lonely, too. And we found each other." He hung his head again. "And now I've lost her."

Jenny had serious doubts about all this. But her friend looked so pitiful. She murmured with real sympathy, "Oh, Nick. I'm so sorry."

He let out a low, sad, moany sound.

She decided they should try to look on the bright side. "Come on. You'll find someone else. You always do."

He lifted his hanging head and met her eyes. "No. That's not the point. I don't just want *someone else.*"

"Well, of course you don't, but—"

He didn't let her finish. Jumping to his feet, he loomed over her. "I pulled myself up from nothing, Jen. And now I'm what they call a success. But it's kind of empty, you know? The single life just ain't what it used to be for me."

She stared up at him and he stared back, expectantly. As if he was waiting for her to comment. When she didn't, he fervently declared, "I want a wife, I admit it." He turned, took a few steps toward the patio doors and then spun back to face her. "I want a wife and kids." He paused, raised both arms and then dropped them to his sides.

Jenny tugged her sweatshirt farther over her knees and said the only thing that came to her. "Well, okay, then."

"No," he argued. "No, Jen. It's not okay. Not okay at all. Hell, Jen. Don't you get it? She has to be the right kind of wife. Sensitive. Smart. Well educated. In one word—Sasha. She has to be Sasha."

"Oh. I see."

"Sasha." He said the name again, with great passion. And then he started pacing back and forth across the section of carpet in front of the coffee table. "Jen, she's the woman I want to spend the rest of my life with. And tonight, after I gave up trying to get drunk, I started thinking. I mean really thinking." He paused and turned to Jenny again.

She could see that he expected her to say something encouraging. So she obliged. "Good for you."

He nodded. "I thought about how I hate my house and I thought how I needed to talk to you. And I also decided that I have to change. I have to...get sensitive. Get romantic. Get to be the kind of man Sasha will be proud to say yes to. You hear what I'm saying, Jen? Do you understand what I'm trying to tell you?"

"Certainly. I do understand. But Nick..."

"What?" He strode back to his end of the couch again and dropped down. "Say it. Go ahead."

"Well, you...can't be someone you're not."

The fervent gleam faded from his eyes. Now he *really* looked wounded. "So you think I'm an insensitive, hard-hatted lunkhead, too, huh?"

"Oh, stop it." She waved a hand at him. "Of course I don't think that, not at all. I only meant that I really can't see you settled down permanently with the woman you just described. But I know you have a good heart. And you've been absolutely wonderful to me and Polly.'' And he had been. More than wonderful. He had been the kind of friend few women are lucky enough to find, right there at her side through Andrew's funeral, and the trial that had put Andrew's killer behind bars for the rest of his life. And he hadn't stopped there. Since then, he was always there whenever she needed him. He was the one Jenny called first when the hot-water heater broke and made the garage into a minilake, the one who would come right over if her stove or her garbage disposal went on the fritz. The one who took Polly to basketball games she didn't want to go to, because he felt it was important that Andrew's daughter learn to appreciate the things her father had loved.

Nick was watching her. He must have known the direction of her thoughts, because a way-too-charming grin was spreading slowly across his face. ''So. You owe me. Right?''

She knew then that he was up to something. He hadn't come to her house at two a.m. just to cry on her shoulder. ''I know that grin.'' She gathered her legs in closer, shrank back against her arm of the couch. ''And I don't like it.''

He slid his arm onto the back of the couch and moved in closer, hemming her in. ''I just figured out how you can pay me back.''

''Nick. I said I don't like this.''

He made a pouty face. ''Don't you want to pay me back?''

''Well, of course. You know I'd do just about anything for you, but—''

"Anything?" The black eyebrows rose and the dark eyes gleamed.

Looking at him, Jenny felt such warmth, such abiding affection—and she knew he was after something every bit as impossible as Sasha, the book-loving art therapist with the fat cat. "Nick, come on."

"Listen. Just listen. You haven't even let me say what it is yet."

"Oh, Nick."

"Don't *Oh, Nick* me. Just listen. Just give me a chance." He jumped to his feet again, stuck his hands into his pockets, pulled them out and gestured widely, with a sweep of both hands. "I know what I need, Jen. I know what's required. And I know you're the one to do it. I mean, you're my friend, so you know all about me. You're going to know right away the areas where I need the most work. And you're a woman, so you're going to be an expert in what I need to learn. And on top of all that, you're a teacher. That is your *job*. You work with fourth-graders, all day long, pounding into their pointy little heads whatever fourth-graders are supposed to know. I guess what I'm saying is, if you can teach fourth-graders, then you can teach me."

"Teach you *what?*"

And he told her. "How to be sensitive and understanding. How to really relate to a woman. How to get in touch with my feminine side and my inner child. How to—"

She was shaking her head. "Nick. No."

But he was nodding. "Jen. Yes. That's what I want from you. That's how you can pay me back. Because I've figured out what's wrong with me. I need to be *trained.*"

Chapter Two

Jenny balked, as Nick had pretty much figured she would. She shrank back to her own side of the couch and she groaned, "*Train* you?"

Nick didn't let her reluctance get him down. He scooted even closer to her and kind of leaned over her, thinking that maybe he could overwhelm her with his enthusiasm, not to mention his size. "Yeah. Train me. Make me into the kind of man Sasha would want for her husband."

Jen faked a glare, narrowing those pretty blue eyes of hers and making her soft, wide mouth into a grim line. "Nick. Get back to your own side of the couch. And do it now."

He stayed nose to nose with her for a count of five, just because it was so much fun to be there. Then he shrugged. "Sure, Jen." And he backed off.

She was quiet, over there hugging the opposite couch arm. He shot her a glance. She glanced back, furtively, trying to read him, trying to figure out how to get him to drop this scheme—which he was not going to do. Finally she said, "This idea is a really bad one, Nick."

"No, it's not."

"Nick, I would have no idea how to do what you're asking. You're a grown man, way past the stage of *training*."

"No, that's not true. I'm only thirty-three. I can still learn. I can be *trained*. Just last year, I took that course in computer assisted drafting, remember? I got some *training*. And I got an *A*, too."

"It's not the same, Nick."

"Why not?"

"Oh, Nick." She let out one of those deep, woman-type sighs, a sigh that managed to hint at everything and tell him nothing, both at the same time.

"There." He snapped his fingers and pointed at her. "That's it."

"*What's* it?"

"The way you said that, 'Oh, Nick,' and then you sighed. I know that was supposed to mean something. If I had some training in how to get along better with women, I would know *what*. I could be *sensitive* and *understanding*. I could *relate* to you the way you need to be related to."

He could see by the set of that strong Swedish jaw of hers that she wasn't buying. "I've got no complaints, Nick. You relate to me just fine."

She could be so damn stubborn sometimes. "Jen,

I'm not talking about you, specifically. I'm talking about *women*. I'm talking about Sasha.''

"Then it's Sasha you should be talking *to* about this.''

"You read that note. How can I talk to Sasha when she doesn't want to see me anymore?''

Jen just looked at him, wearing one of those how-do-I get-through-to-you expressions. Then she unwrapped her stretched-out sweatshirt from around her knees and stood. She started picking up the photo albums. Nick knew what that meant. First, came the picking up. Then she would be shooing him out into the cold, dark night. She turned with the albums, carried them across the room and put them away in a cabinet at the base of one of the bookcases.

When she marched back over, scooped up her wineglass and started toward the steps that led up to the dining area and the kitchen, he decided he needed to try a little begging. "Jen. Please. I want to change. I'm ready to change. And you could help me to change.''

She paused with her foot on the bottom step. "If you want to change, you will.''

He put all his heart into looking really pitiful. "Aw, Jen.''

Naturally she relented—at least a little bit. "Look. I'll do some thinking about it, okay? Maybe I can recommend some self-help books or something. And I'll see if I can dig up some kind of therapy group you could get into.''

He gulped at that one. "Therapy? You think I need a shrink?''

She'd started for the kitchen again, but then turned

back. "Nick. Stop it. I don't think you *need* anything. I think you're just fine the way you are."

That made him feel better. "You do?"

"Yes. I think you are an extremely capable and focused man. And if you've decided that you want a wife, you'll find her. You should just give it a little time—and maybe look for a new place to meet women, because a woman who goes to the Nine-Seventeen Club is probably not looking for a partner in life."

That remark bugged him a little. He defended himself. "I told you, I went there because I was lonely. And Sasha was—"

"I know, I know. Sasha was lonely, too. Nick, it's all right. There's nothing wrong with a singles bar. I was only suggesting that you might find another place to look for a wife." Since he couldn't come up with an immediate reply to that, she turned and made her escape. There was a counter to his left, with stools beneath it and a pass-through into the kitchen, so he could hear her in there, running the water, rinsing out that wineglass. He even heard the little clink as she set the glass down.

Then she was back, standing over him. "Nick. It's late."

He thought about his house, about the way the huge rooms echoed, especially late at night, and he stared up at her, putting on the pitiful look again. "Don't make me go back to that house of mine. I just can't take it tonight. And tomorrow is *Sunday,* Jenny. Waking up Sunday morning in that house of mine is the worst."

"Maybe you should move, then."

"Maybe I should. But that doesn't help me tonight."

She pressed her lips together, looking exactly like the schoolteacher she was. All she needed was a pair of those old-lady half-glasses perched on the end of her nose. He thought of what it must be like, to be one of her fourth-graders. That she would be strict, but she'd have a heart with the troublemakers, too.

"Just a pillow and a blanket," he coaxed. "I'll stretch out right here."

She made a little *tsking* sound, with her tongue against the back of her teeth, and then she turned, marched up the steps, through the dining room and down the hall. She reappeared a moment later with a big, soft quilt and a pillow.

She tossed the bedding at him and he caught it. "Thanks, Jen."

"You can use the futon in the spare room."

Nick hated that damn futon. He'd slept on it three or four times over the years. It had a mattress like a large, flat rock. "Thanks. Right here will be just fine."

"Polly will probably be up early."

"Good. I'll get to see her before I leave."

Jen wrapped her arms around her middle and rubbed at one stockinged foot with the toes of the other. "Nick. I do...wish that what you wanted was something I could really help you with. Because you honestly are the best friend a woman could have."

"So." He gave her a wink. "Maybe there's hope for me, huh?"

A soft smile lifted the corners of her mouth and lit up her eyes. "Oh, I think so. Definitely. I think that whatever you want, you'll figure out a way to get eventually. And if this Sasha really is the one for you, she'd better come to her senses right away and realize what a lucky woman she is.''

That gave him an idea. "Hey. Maybe you could give her a call. You could tell her—''

"Nick. Good night.'' Her expression said he'd better not push his luck.

So he didn't. "Night, Jen.''

Jenny turned and headed down the hall.

The next morning, Jenny woke at a few minutes after eight, which was late for her. She tossed back the covers, swung her feet to the carpet and went to open the wood blinds that covered her bedroom window.

The sun was out, which cheered her. On that day exactly four years ago, the sky had been overcast, steely gray with high fog.

Next to the rim of ivy that grew close to the back fence, a scruffy-looking robin jumped around on the lawn. Jenny smiled as she watched the bird peck the cold ground, ruffle its feathers and then tip its throat back and warble a brief song. Then, finished warbling and pecking, the robin flew off, taking flight into the blue sky and disappearing from her sight.

Jenny turned from the window. Her leggings and sweatshirt lay across the corner chair. She reached for them.

When she emerged from her bedroom a few minutes later, she found Nick and Polly at the oval-shaped oak dining table. The winter sunlight bled down through the skylight over their heads. Jenny and Andrew had scrimped and saved to get that skylight. Nick had put it in for them, just before Andrew's death, to lighten the area that had always seemed too dark, since it lay in the heart of the house, surrounded by other rooms.

Nick sat in Andrew's place, at the end of the table. Polly sat where she always sat, in the curve of the oval, right next to him. They had their heads together, silvered black and chestnut brown.

Jenny remembered other mornings, remembered Andrew spooning up Grape-Nuts, and a much-younger Polly, babbling away to her father, her own breakfast cereal getting soggy in the bowl because she'd rather talk than eat. Jenny's heart contracted. Her loss felt suddenly achingly fresh—an old wound reopened.

Polly glanced up and saw her mother standing in the entrance to the hall. Nick looked over, too.

"Hey," Nick said. "I made the coffee and brought in the Sunday *Bee*."

"Great," Jenny chirped, forcing a brightness she didn't feel at that moment. Briskly she strode on past them, heading for the kitchen, needing a minute or two to get her emotions back under control.

Jenny got down her favorite mug from the cabinet. In the other room, Polly started talking to Nick. "Okay, listen. I want you to read the Erica Jong poems right away. They'll give you some idea about how a woman really feels." Her voice was low and confidential, full of authority and something else—excitement, yes, that was it. Jenny filled her mug as Polly continued, "And you can just glance through those *Woman's Day*s and *Cosmopolitan*s. Look for the articles about relationships, you know? Things like how to communicate with the people you love and how to keep love alive when you've been married forever, okay? Oh, and buy some CDs by Enya and Celine Dion. Women your age really go for that stuff.''

Jenny heard Nick grunt, a sound that seemed to indicate agreement.

Sipping her coffee, Jenny turned the wand that opened the blinds to the window over the sink. The sun came in, having cleared the rooftops now. It shone through the winter-bare branches of the fruitless mulberry tree in the center of the lawn.

From behind her, Polly was giving further instructions to Nick. ''And read the *Sonnets from the Portuguese*. It's pure woman's passion, from a woman's point of view. As you read those, we'll talk about them. In depth.''

Jenny had heard enough. She turned from the window and marched to the table. Now she'd gotten past her moment of self-pity at the sight of Nick sitting in Andrew's place, she saw what she hadn't noticed before: a stack of books to Nick's left, a pile of magazines to his right and a batch of videos dead center. Both Nick and Polly were looking at her again—Nick, rather sheepishly, Polly with impatience.

''What, Mom?'' her daughter demanded.

Jenny pulled out the chair next to Polly and sat. ''What is going on?''

Polly sat back in her chair, folded her arms over her still-flat chest and announced with way too much disdain, ''Nick has come to me for help. And *I'm* not going to let him down.''

Jenny sipped more coffee, glancing from Polly to Nick and back to Polly once more. Then she set the mug down and massaged her temples. ''Nick, what have you been telling her?''

"Now, Jen, I just—"

Polly didn't let him finish. With an irritable little snorting sound, she interrupted, "Nick told me that he's in love, Mother. With a woman named Sasha. And that he wants to *change*. I think it's…beautiful, that he wants to understand a woman's needs. And I am going to help him."

Jenny looked at her daughter, at the slim nose and green eyes she got from Andrew. At the unsmiling mouth—which was full of braces she always tried to hide—and at the stubborn jaw so much like Jenny's own. The urge came hard to ask, *And what, exactly, does a thirteen-year-old know about a woman's needs?*

Jenny restrained that urge. Polly would only react with adolescent outrage if she did. She spoke gently. "Honey, I really don't think—"

This time Nick was the one who didn't let her finish. "Come on, Jen. What can it hurt? The worst that can happen is I'll read a few good books, right?"

Polly chimed in again, loftily now, "And just maybe he'll end up with the woman of his dreams." She put her hand on Jenny's forearm and she lowered her voice to a drone of great solemnity. "Mom. Nick is our friend. And people help their friends."

Jenny looked into her daughter's eyes and immediately felt herself weakening. Those eyes—Andrew's eyes—fairly danced with anticipation at the prospect of "training" Nick to be worthy of the elusive Sasha Overfield.

How long had it been since Polly had become really excited about anything? Too long. Back in August, Polly's best pal, Amelia Gordon, had moved across town to a big, expensive house in Greenhaven. Ever since then, Polly spent too much time in her room, writing in the blank books she used as journals, listening to Robynn Carllson and Vivaldi on her Walkman and reading good literature that was probably too mature for her.

As Nick had just said, what harm could it do? And there might be a real benefit to this silliness, if helping Nick with his "problem" brought a general improvement in Polly's attitude.

Of course, beyond being silly, the scheme was more than likely utterly futile. The Sacramento Kings would make the NBA Finals before Nick DeSalvo was ever going to read a whole book of nineteenth-century love sonnets. And beyond its impossibility, the whole thing felt wrong, somehow. Probably because this Sasha woman seemed totally unsuited to Nick, anyway. Why should he make himself over to try to please a woman with whom he had nothing in common?

"Mom." Polly squeezed her arm. *"Please."*

"Yeah." Nick put in his two cents. "Come on, Jen. Give us a chance here."

Jenny looked from her daughter to Andrew's friend, who had become *her* friend. Nick's deep-set dark eyes held the same appeal as Polly's leaf green ones. How could she fight them both?

And why should she even want to, really? The worst that could happen was what probably *would* happen: Nick would quickly lose interest—and for a little while, Polly would be a pure trial to live with as she sulked over his lack of dedication to her plan.

"Mom?" Impatience had found its way back into Polly's voice. "Nick needs this. Let me help him."

Nick said nothing more. He just waited.

And Jenny heard herself agreeing, "Oh, all right. Why not?"

Chapter Three

"All I'm saying is, it seems like a lot of whining to me," Nick grumbled. "A lot of whining that doesn't even rhyme. I mean, come on." He held up the book of sonnets and read, "'Oh, Beloved, it is plain I am not of thy worth nor for thy place!'" He grunted. "Whining. Damn confusing whining. Exactly what does this woman *mean?*"

Polly was only too eager to enlighten him. She explained in her best intellectual tone, "In this sonnet, the eleventh, Elizabeth Barrett reveals her fears of unworthiness for Robert Browning's love. She feels she's just not good enough for him, and so she renounces him."

"Oh, well now. That makes a damn lot of sense."

At the oven a few feet away, Jenny smiled to herself as she checked on the potatoes. It was Wednesday, the third day of Nick's "training." So far, he was sticking with it—but griping all the way.

Nick continued, "Neither of them are married to anyone else, right? And she wants him and he wants her. She writes poems and so does he."

"So?" Polly demanded, sounding put out.

"So, they like the same things and they wouldn't be cheating on anybody. What's the damn problem?"

"I told you, Nick. She feels like she's not good enough for him. He's a man of the world and she's barely ever left her house."

"Then she should get out more. He could help her with that."

"Nick. She's shy. And she's been sick a lot."

"And that's *his* fault?"

"No." Polly spoke with admirable patience. "But she's very *sensitive*. She's afraid she won't fit into his world."

"So she's whining about it—and telling him to get lost. What the hell good is that going to do either of them?"

"Oh, Nick..." Polly was shaking her head; Jenny knew that without having to turn and look.

Jenny shut the oven door, "Dinner in ten minutes. Polly, you'd better get the table set."

Polly huffed in exasperation. "Mother, we just got started here and we have a lot of work to do."

"Yes, honey. But you also have to eat."

Nick had already jumped to his feet. He began gathering up the books and magazines the two of them had spread out on the table. "Come on, Pol. I'll help you." He shot Jenny a hopeful glance. "Sure smells good."

She knew what he was after. Somehow, the past

three nights, he always managed to arrive just in time for dinner. "All right. You may stay."

He beamed. "Great."

He and Polly set the table. Then the three of them sat down and ate the meal Jenny had prepared. Then Nick cleared the table and he and Polly cleaned up the dishes. Jenny headed for the spare room and her desk there. She had a few papers to correct.

The phone rang at seven-thirty. It was Amelia Gordon. Jenny called for her daughter and Polly yelled back, "I'll get it in my room!"

Polly's footsteps pounded down the hall. Then her bedroom door slammed. Jenny winced and sighed and wondered why Polly never did anything in moderation lately. The girl either ran and slammed doors—or she dragged around moaning that her life was just too boring for words.

"That would be Amelia, right?" Nick was standing in the doorway to the hall.

"Yep." Jenny tossed her red marker aside and turned her swivel chair around to face him. "My guess is that the training session's over for tonight."

"Yeah. You're probably right." He leaned on the door frame and ran both hands back over his hair, in that characteristic gesture that somehow always made her feel fond of him. "I was getting pretty sick of that Barrett woman anyway."

She couldn't resist teasing, "Probably because you're not in touch with your feminine self. Yet."

"Right. That must be it." He looked at her sideways, and then he pulled himself away from the door frame and came fully into the room with her.

She watched him, thinking that she had work to do,

that he ought to be making see-you-later noises and going on his way.

He dropped to the futon, which was folded into the couch position, against the wall to her left. She swiveled his way and watched him draw in a long breath through his nose.

"What?" she asked.

"Nothing." He draped both powerful arms along the top of the backrest. "Your house always smells good, that's all."

She crossed one leg over the other, clasped her hands around her raised knee and made a show of sniffing the air. "Smells like the dinner we ate a while ago and that's about all."

"Exactly. Oven-browned potatoes. Cube steak. White gravy. My house never smells like that."

She leaned forward and lowered her voice a notch, though Polly was in the other room with her door shut, sharing secrets with Amelia, and doubtless couldn't hear a thing Jenny said. "Nick. Is this about Sasha? Do you want to talk about her?"

He shrugged. "No, not particularly. What's to say?" For a moment, he looked sad. But then his expression brightened. "I just like it here. I wanted you to know."

She felt pleased—and somehow wary at the same time. "Well. I'm glad. Thank you."

He lowered one arm and patted the mattress. "The first time I slept on this thing, that was…what, ten years ago now?"

"Closer to twelve years, I think." The first time Nick had slept on the futon had been in the apartment over on Howe Avenue, where Jenny and Andrew had lived until they'd finally scraped enough together to put a down payment on the house. In the apartment, the futon had served as both living room sofa and guest bed.

Nick chuckled low, remembering. "I was just starting out, just got my general contractor's license. I'd bid lower than low on some job—and still lost out. I was steamed."

"So you got drunk."

"Drunk as a skunk."

"And then you showed up at our place."

"You were mad."

"Well…"

"You were. You didn't like me much then."

"You didn't like me much, either."

"Yeah, well. The minute Andy met you—in that English class, wasn't it?"

She nodded. "Honors English. Junior year of high school."

"Right. The minute he met you it was 'Jenny this' and 'Jenny that.' I was jealous as hell. Even if you both did have a lot in common—both being A students, both wanting to be teachers—I still couldn't see any reason why my best bud in the damn world should be spending so much time with one female. Then he proved my point—or so I thought at the time."

"How?"

"He went and married you straight out of high school. And then, boom, not even a year later, there was Polly. I thought he'd messed up his life but good."

"It never occurred to you that we both just knew what we wanted?"

"Are you kidding? Nobody knows what they want straight out of high school."

"Translation: *You* didn't know what you wanted straight out of high school."

He picked up a little pillow with a crocheted cover on it and held it to his chest, casting his dark gaze toward the textured ceiling overhead. "The woman knows me too well." He looked at her again. "But really. Look at my folks. They were both eighteen when they got married. And they hit the divorce courts when I was ten." Nick's mother had finished raising him on her own, scraping and struggling to get by. She had died seven years ago, "Of a bad attitude and plain overwork," Nick always claimed. His father had moved away from Sacramento. He lived in Oregon somewhere. He and Nick didn't keep in touch.

"Anyway," Nick said. "You didn't like me any better than I liked you. You couldn't understand why Andy would want to hang around with a *drunken macho moron* like me."

Jenny hid a smile and tried to look innocent. "Did I call you that?"

"You did. Those exact words. That night I showed up drunk at your apartment. You dragged poor Andy aside and you said, 'I mean it, Andrew, get that drunken macho moron out of here before he wakes up Polly.'"

Jenny looked down at her clasped hands. "I didn't mean for you to hear."

Nick chuckled some more. "I know. But I did. I really felt like I got one up on you when Andy didn't have the heart to throw me out. He just told me to keep it down. And then he let me sleep on the futon."

Nick set the pillow against the backrest and patted it once, shooting Jenny a sideways glance. "I didn't turn out to be so bad, after all—did I?"

"No," she told him honestly, still wondering what he really had on his mind. "You turned out to be just terrific."

"—And I guess you're wondering what the hell I'm after now."

At last, she thought. "I guess I am."

"Well, what are you doing Saturday night?"

She sat a little straighter, feeling more wary by the second. "Why, what's going on Saturday night?"

"A fund-raiser for disadvantaged kids. Over at the Hyatt Regency. Drinks, dinner, dancing. A few speeches. Sasha was going to go with me, but now…" He let a shrug finish the thought. "And I can't just send a check to this one. The wife of one of the major investors on my latest project put the whole thing together. I told her I'd be there."

"Are you sure you can't just go to this event alone?"

He gave her an extremely patient look. "Come on, Jen. A guy doesn't show up stag to something like this. And if I can't take Sasha…" He shuffled his boots, sat forward and then sat back again. "I got out my address book, you hear what I'm saying? I started thumbing through it. And there wasn't a phone number in there I wanted to call." He punched at the little crocheted pillow again.

Watching him, Jenny wondered if she'd taken this whole Sasha thing too lightly, if she'd been so wrapped up in the grim job of getting past another anniversary of Andrew's death that she hadn't really given Nick the support and understanding he'd needed the other night.

She asked gently, "Nick, are you going to be all right?"

He made a low noise in his throat, then gave her his cockiest grin. "Hell, yes. I'll be fine. I'm just…going through a few changes, I guess. And I'm not in the mood to take some woman I couldn't care less about to a fancy gig at the Hyatt Regency. I'd rather take you. If I took you, I might even have a little damn fun."

His words warmed her. And why was she hesitating anyway? She might have a little fun, too. She'd put on her slinkiest dress and be treated to a meal that she didn't have to cook herself.

But then again, how many slinky dresses did she own? It had been years, literally, since she'd attended the kind of function Nick was describing. The closest thing to it was probably the New Year's Eve bash she and Andrew had gone to shortly before he died. To that, she'd worn a basic black number, which had been hanging in the deepest recesses of her closet ever since. It probably had moth holes in it by now.

"Why the big frown?" Nick demanded. "It can't be that depressing to think of spending Saturday night with me—can it?"

She couldn't resist teasing, "Well, it does sound like quite a chore."

He sat forward and peered at her closely. Then he straightened his broad shoulders and announced, "That's a yes. I know it. You'll do it, won't you?"

"Oh, all right. I suppose I will."

He leapt up, grabbed her hands and yanked her out

of her swivel chair. His big arms went around her and he pulled her up close. "Aw, Jen. You're a pal."

Jenny smiled against his chest. She felt safe and protected, the way she had the other night, when he'd embraced her to comfort her about Andrew. She slid her arms around him and hugged him back.

Cradled close against him, she found herself remembering the day the verdict came in on the man who'd murdered Andrew in the doughnut shop holdup.

They'd given her a seat in the front row of the spectator's section. Her mother sat on her right, and Nick on her left. Andrew's father and mother were a little farther down the row.

The judge asked, "Foreperson White, have you reached a verdict?"

The jury foreman said, "Yes."

Jenny had held her breath in fierce desire for the sound of one word: guilty.

But it didn't come. Instead they started passing forms around—from the foreman to the bailiff and then to the judge. The judge had studied the forms, taking a minute or two that to Jenny had seemed like forever and a day.

During that endless, agonizing wait, Nick reached out. His big hand covered hers, enfolding it in warmth and strength and total understanding.

The judge passed the forms to the court clerk.

The clerk began to read. "In the Superior Court of the State of California, in and for the County of Sacramento, case number..."

To Jenny, the words had all blurred together into one continuous hum. Hot tears stung her eyes. Her body was rigid, so stiff it ached, while her heart rose up high in her chest, cutting off her air. She twined her fingers with Nick's and held on tight.

The clerk reached the first charge, that of murder in the second degree, with special circumstances. Jenny heard some numbers from the penal code. And then that single, blessed word she understood.

"Guilty."

Down the row, Andrew's mother cried out. Jenny's own mother gasped. Jenny's heart dropped back to its proper place and started beating once again. A single tear escaped her control and trailed down her cheek just as Nick's big, warm hand gave hers a triumphant squeeze....

Jenny knew she was letting the hug go on too long. Gently she pushed at Nick's broad chest.

He immediately released her and stepped back. "Okay. I know you've got work to do. And I'm getting out of your hair right now." He started for the door to the hall.

Just before he went through it, she remembered to ask, "What time?"

He glanced back at her. "Huh?"

"What time will you pick me up?"

"Seven-thirty?"

"Sounds good."

"Thanks, Jen." He saluted her with a hand to his forehead, and then he went out through the hall. She stared after him for a moment, thinking about that black dress in the back of her closet, telling herself she'd have to dig it out and look it over later tonight or tomorrow. The front door opened and closed. She turned with a sigh to the papers waiting on her desk.

A while later, just as Jenny was marking a grade on

the final paper in the stack, Polly spoke from behind her. "Where'd Nick go?"

Jenny capped her red marker and turned enough to look over her shoulder at her daughter. "Home, I'd imagine."

Polly brushed a hank of hair back from her face and let out a groan. "But I *told* him I'd be back."

Jenny glanced at the little travel clock, which sat on a shelf in the top part of the high-backed desk. It had been almost an hour since Polly had disappeared into her room.

Polly saw the direction of her mother's gaze and immediately jumped into defensive mode. "Mother. Amelia *is* my best friend. And she *needed* me tonight. So when she called, we had to talk a little longer than I expected."

"Oh? What did you *have* to talk about?"

Polly stubbed the toe of her shoe against the carpet. "I can't tell you everything, not anymore. Mellie had a *personal* problem."

"Well, fine. You dealt with Amelia's problem. And Nick went home." Jenny picked up the stack of papers and tapped them on the desk, to straighten them. Then she bent to scoop up her briefcase. A moment later, she'd popped the latches and was sliding the corrected papers into one of the pouches that lined the lid. That accomplished, she snapped the briefcase shut again and set it back against the side of the desk. "How's your homework situation?"

"Handled."

Jenny didn't doubt her daughter's word on that subject. Polly might run down the hall, slam doors and forget all about poor Nick and his training session the minute the phone rang, but she took her schoolwork seriously. She always brought home report cards loaded with A's.

Jenny switched off the green-shaded desk lamp and stood, pressing at the small of her back, stretching, working out the kinks from sitting for an hour and a half.

Polly still lingered in the doorway. Now she looked contrite. "Did Nick seem mad, when he left?"

Jenny felt a little tug in the vicinity of her heart. She'd been thirteen herself once, and prone to thoughtlessness—which she'd always regretted later. She told her daughter softly, "He didn't seem mad at all to me."

Polly smiled, broadly for once, showing her relief—as well as the braces she hated so much. She confessed, "But I guess it was kind of rude, huh, to just go off and leave him like that?"

"I'd say it was something I wouldn't do again, if I were you."

"I won't."

"Good." Jenny crossed the small room and turned off the overhead light at the switch right beside the door.

Polly trailed along after her as she headed for her bedroom. "Oh, Mother. Do you think I'm making progress with him?"

In her own room, Jenny turned on the big floor lamp by her dresser. "You mean Nick?"

Polly dropped onto Jenny's bed, then flopped onto her back with a drawn-out sigh. "Who else?"

Jenny turned for her closet, pausing once she got there to remark, "Well, he's reading those love sonnets, isn't he? That's something. I never believed for a minute you'd get him to do that.''

Polly folded her hands over her middle and stared up at the ceiling. ''That's true. Too bad all he ever does is complain when we talk about them.''

Jenny pushed back the mirrored closet door. ''If he's reading them, that's something. And yesterday you had that nice discussion about that *Cosmopolitan* article.''

''Right. 'What To Do When Good Love Goes Bad.' I guess he could relate to that, with the Sasha situation and everything. I mean, I *think* I'm making progress. I'm doing my best. But with Nick, it's hard to tell.''

''Be patient, honey. It's only been a few days.''

''I know, but…you know how he always jokes about things? I tell him to watch a romantic movie and he says, 'How 'bout *Rebound Masters of the NBA?*''' She imitated Nick's deep voice. '''That romantic enough for ya?'''

Jenny heard her daughter from a distance now. She'd stuck her head in the closet and begun shoving at hangers, looking for the black dress. Finally she spotted it, all the way in the back. ''Ah-ha!'' She reached for it and dragged it out.

Polly rolled her head to look when Jenny emerged from the closet. ''What's that?''

Jenny gathered up the plastic and eased it off the hanger. ''Your basic little black dress—evening version.'' Holding the dress against herself with the hanger under her chin, she turned so she could see herself in the mirrored closet door. ''What do you think?''

Polly sat up. ''Mother. What is going on?''

''Oh, Nick has some charity dinner and dance he

can't get out of this Saturday.'' Jenny tossed the wad-ded-up plastic cover onto the little chair in the corner and then moved to the bed to lay the dress down where she could examine it more closely. "He asked me if I'd go with him.''

Polly hitched in a small gasp, then demanded in ut-ter disbelief, "You mean like a *date?*''

Jenny picked up the hem of the dress and brushed away a bit of lint that clung there. "Well, let's put it this way. He was going to take Sasha, but you know about Sasha.''

"Right. So?''

"So he decided he wanted to go with a friend.'' Jenny put her hand against her throat and smiled with appropriate modesty. "That would be me.''

Polly was looking at her as if she had mustard on her nose—too closely, but hesitating to mention it. "So it's just a 'friend' thing.''

"Right.'' Jenny picked up the dress and turned it over, smoothing it out, checking for moth holes or pulled threads.

Polly said nothing for a moment, then asked, "Mom?''

"Mmm?''

"This could be useful.''

Jenny glanced up. "Useful?''

"Yes. Don't you see? You'll have to report back to me. Tell me *everything*.''

"About what?''

"About Nick, silly. About how he behaves on a date. Then, later, I can give him a few pointers on—''

Jenny put up a hand, palm out. "Whoa.''

Polly widened those pretty green eyes. "What?''

"I am not going to spend my evening checking on Nick to make sure he knows which fork to use. He has done quite well for himself, in case you weren't aware. The man knows how to behave at a social event."

The corners of Polly's mouth pulled down in her best I-am-gravely-offended expression. "Mother, that is not what I meant."

"Well, whatever you meant, *don't.* This whole 'training' thing is between you and Nick. I didn't say no to it because you both seemed so excited about giving it a try. But do not expect me to get involved. Understand?"

"Oh, *Mother.*"

"*Understand?*"

"Yeah. Sure. Gotcha." Polly flopped to her back again and stared at the ceiling some more. "Sheesh," she said, then muttered with great sarcasm, "I hope you have a *marvelous* time."

"Thank you very much, I think I will. And I'll ask your grandmother to come and stay with you, just so you won't be alone."

Polly sniffed. "I'm thirteen years old. I'll be fine." Then she turned her head, sarcasm forgotten. "Hey. Maybe I could have Mellie over. To spend the night. We wouldn't need Granny, then."

Jenny marveled sometimes at the workings of her daughter's mind. If she hesitated to leave one thirteen-year-old alone, what led Polly to believe that she'd feel better if she left *two?*

"Mom. *Please?*"

"If your grandma's here to keep an eye on you, having Mellie over would be fine."

"We do not need Granny."

"I'm the mom here. I'll decide what you need."

"Oh, great. Whatever. Fine." Polly dragged herself to a standing position. "So. Can I call Mellie and invite her?"

"Let me talk to your grandmother first."

"When will you do that?"

"Tomorrow, I promise."

Grumbling under her breath, Polly wandered back to her own room.

Alone, Jenny tried on the dress. It looked fine and it still fit. But as she turned before the mirror, she couldn't help thinking that something new would be nice.

Once a week, on Thursday, Polly stayed two hours after school to tutor kids who were having trouble in reading and language arts. Jenny usually spent that time in her own classroom, redoing bulletin boards and straightening supply closets. But that particular Thursday, the bulletin boards didn't need changing—and the supply closets could wait.

Jenny got in her car and drove to Arden Fair Mall. Luck must have been shining on her, because she found a parking space in a row right near one of the entrances to Nordstrom's.

She saw the dress hanging on the end of the rack when she got off the escalator onto the second floor. It was turquoise, a sort of peacock turquoise, the color pearlescent, seeming to alter with every change in the light. It was evening length, with a slit up the back to the knee. It had a mandarin collar and cutaway shoulders—and a matching jacket that would ward off the cold night air. Jenny glanced at the price tag. Four hundred and eighty dollars.

She shouldn't.

Still, she found a dressing room and tried it on, her heart pounding in excitement. She loved the way the slinky fabric slid down her body, like water. Water with substance, yes, that was how it felt.

One glance in the mirror and she knew she had to have it.

Of course, she needed a special bra for it. So after the salesclerk rang it up and covered it carefully with a Nordstrom's bag, Jenny went over to lingerie and bought the right bra—along with a pair of shimmery stockings. Her pulse racing, she dared to stop in at the shoe department, where she actually found a pair of turquoise evening sandals.

Her heart was still pounding too hard and too loud as she carried everything back to the car.

She hung the dress in the back seat and put the other things in the trunk. Then she slid behind the wheel.

That was when she realized that her hands were shaking.

She grasped the wheel to steady them. Her heart went on thudding, as loud as a barrel drum. The sound seemed to fill the car. Jenny gritted her teeth, gripped the wheel harder and stared out the windshield.

"I have just spent six hundred dollars," Jenny said aloud to no one in particular. She said it again, "I have just spent six hundred dollars." This time, she added, "To go out on Saturday night. With Nick."

Chapter Four

With a tiny moan, Jenny leaned on her door and got out of the car. A cold wind was blowing. It lifted her pale hair and blew it against her cheeks as she locked the car and then hurried back into the mall.

She wandered around for a few minutes, staring blindly at display windows, and then found a pizza stand. She bought a giant-sized Diet Pepsi and she sat at a table by herself. Slowly she sipped, watching the people go by in the mall a few feet away.

At the next table over, a young man and woman were sharing a pizza with a small, blond-haired child.

"Drink your milk now, Lily," the woman said.

The little girl lifted her paper cup and took a big sip, then set the cup down and pointed at her upper lip. "Moustache, Mommy," she announced with great pride. The man took a napkin and swiped at the little girl's mouth. Childish giggles rang out. "All clean now, Daddy?"

"All clean. Drink the rest."

Obediently the child drank some more.

Jenny tried not to be too obvious about watching them, a happy little family, sharing pizza at the mall. Once, she and Andrew and Polly might have been in their place.

It did hurt to see them. To remember how it had once been, but could never be again.

Still, it didn't hurt as much as it would have at one time.

Jenny supposed she took comfort from that.

Plus, the more she thought about it, the more she realized that even if Andrew were still with them, it could hardly be the same. Polly wouldn't be crowing over a milk moustache, not by a long shot. And Andrew certainly wouldn't be wiping her mouth for her.

Jenny sipped from her straw, and let herself think again of the dress hanging in the back seat of her car. If spending the money bothered her so much, she could always march back out there collect everything, and return it all right now. She could wear the black one. It was thoroughly appropriate for the occasion.

But her hands weren't shaking anymore. And her heart had settled down. She saw her earlier reaction as just what it had been: an *over*reaction.

In the first months after Andrew's death, she'd had reactions like that often. Her heart would go crazy and her hands would shake—over the simplest things, in the most mundane places. Once, in the grocery store, she'd rolled her cart by the condiment section and realized she didn't need to buy mayonnaise that day.

Neither she nor Polly cared for it; it was Andrew who put the stuff on everything, going through a giant jar every month, at least. She used to tease him about it, telling him she could hear his arteries hardening as he spread that stuff on thick.

But that day in the grocery store, she realized she wouldn't be teasing him anymore. Nope. And she didn't need to buy mayonnaise, that was for sure. And all at once, her hands were shaking. And her heart pounded so hard, it hurt to have it beating in there.

She saw herself, stepping right up to that shelf, calmly reaching for those jars of mayonnaise, one by one and hurling them to the floor of the aisle, shattering them all, each and every one, till the store was awash in mayonnaise and greasy shards of broken glass.

She'd left her cart right there in the middle of the aisle and gone out and sat in her car for a full five minutes before she made herself go back inside and finish the shopping she'd started.

She had told herself that what mattered was that she *had* finished what she'd started.

And every time she bought groceries after that, it got a little easier, until she could walk by the condiment section with no escalation of her pulse at all, without even glancing at the mayonnaise jars.

Maybe she *had* spent too much on the dress. But it had been so long since she'd bought a dress just because she wanted to, just because she saw it on the rack and knew that it was meant for her. Just because it brought out the hints of pink in her skin, deepened her pale blue eyes. And flowed down her body like water given substance.

Heck, maybe she'd never bought a dress for those particular reasons, now she really gave it some thought.

A pure, sinful self-indulgence, that's what that dress was.

Jenny stood. She left the father, the mother, the little golden-haired daughter and the pizza stand behind. A few yards down the mall, she found a trash can and dropped the remains of her Pepsi into it.

Every woman, she decided, had a right to a pure self-indulgence now and then. As long as she didn't make a habit of it, of course.

Jenny arrived home before Polly. She put her new dress away. She was starting on dinner when the mother of one of the students Polly tutored dropped her off at the foot of the driveway. Jenny watched through the kitchen window as her daughter waved, then turned and ran up the walk.

Polly slammed the front door. "Mom! I'm home!"

"In the kitchen!"

Polly came flying in, cheeks bright red from the cold outside. She dropped her heavy pack on the table and shrugged out of her down jacket. "Test tomorrow in World History." She held up her history book, which she clutched in her hands. "I want to look over the chapter again." She tossed the jacket on top of the pack. "Call me when Nick gets here, okay?"

"Sure."

Polly whirled for the hall.

"Wait."

Polly groaned. "What, Mom?"

"Hang up your jacket. And take that pack to your room."

"Oh, *Mom*..."

Jenny just looked at her. Grumbling under her breath, Polly grabbed up the two articles and disappeared down the hall. Jenny called after her, "And don't slam that—" Before she could finish the sentence, Polly's door slammed.

Shaking her head, Jenny turned for the counter where several stalks of celery and a yellow onion waited to be sliced.

Nick arrived at a little after six, just in time to help Polly set the table. By seven, Polly had him looking at Georgia O'Keeffe calla lilies as well as oils and pastels by Mary Cassatt.

"So you'll have something constructive to contribute," Polly explained to him, "when Sasha wants to talk about art."

Polly pointed out the feminine, sensual lines of the Georgia O'Keeffe flowers. Nick grunted and turned the page, "Hey, this isn't bad." It was a cow skull with a peony growing out of the left eye.

Polly launched into her interpretation of the piece—which didn't seem to make a lot of sense to Nick. He grunted some more.

Jenny retreated to the spare room, where she plunked herself down on the futon and watched "Rivera Live" on the small TV in there. Around nine, she got up and turned off the TV.

Out in the dining area, Nick was getting ready to leave.

"Making progress?" she asked as he pulled on his jacket.

"Ask the teacher," he advised.

Polly said chidingly, "I really don't think you ought to miss tomorrow night, Nick. Monday through Friday, that was the deal, remember? Until we both think you're really getting somewhere."

Nick said, "Look, Pol. I'm sorry. But I've got a meeting that's bound to run late."

"Come over afterward."

"Can't. Gotta get home."

Jenny smiled to herself. She had thumbed through the *TV Guide* a few minutes earlier and noticed that there was a Bulls game on tomorrow night—which was the only reason she could possibly imagine that Nick might be eager to get home to that awful house of his; he had a big-screen TV in the huge living room.

Polly sighed. "Well. Keep up with your reading. Don't slack off."

"I won't."

"Monday we'll discuss *Wuthering Heights*."

"I can't wait."

"Just get it read."

"I will, I will." Nick shot a glance past Polly, at Jenny. "Seven-thirty Saturday, right?"

She thought of the dress, hanging in her closet. Of herself wearing it, dancing in Nick's arms. She didn't know whether she felt elated—or sick to her stomach. "I'll be ready."

"See you then."

Staring at herself in the mirror on her closet door, Jenny straightened the jacket a little and smoothed the fabric of the turquoise dress. She looked fine, she thought. She'd swept the sides of her chin-length blond hair back away from her face. The earrings with the tiny sapphires in them that Andrew had given her for their fifth anniversary sparkled in her ears. She turned, so that she could look back over her shoulder for a rear view.

Yes. Fine. Perfect. No reason to be so nervous. No reason at all.

Laughter drifted to her from down the hall. Her mother and the two girls, Polly and Amelia, had settled in at the table to play something called MindTrap. Of course, the girls had groaned when Granny suggested the game. But Kirsten Lundquist hadn't let the groaning bother her. Like her mother before her and her daughter after, Kirsten Lundquist was a teacher to her bones; she'd taught everything from kindergarten to high school algebra. And she knew how to ignore the complaints of recalcitrant children.

She'd clapped her hands briskly. "Come on, girls. Let's get this table cleared. Then we will enjoy a game that will challenge our minds a little—and allow us to enjoy each other's company at the same time. Meanwhile, Jennifer will have the time she needs to get ready for her big date."

Her big date. Jenny stared at her own reflection in the mirror as her mother's words bounced around in her brain. Her eyes looked way too wide. And her lips too pale.

More lipstick. That should help. She whirled for the mirror over the sink in her bathroom. The lipstick waited there on the edge of the sink, where she'd left it a few minutes before. She grabbed it and pulled off the cap.

And right then, the doorbell rang.

Startled, Jenny emitted a tiny cry of alarm. The lid stayed in one hand, but the lipstick itself went flying. It bounced against the mirror and fell into the sink.

"Ridiculous. Foolish," Jenny muttered to herself as she commanded her hand to stop shaking, picked up the lipstick again, rolled it out, then slowly and carefully applied it to her lips.

"There," she said, rubbing her lips together as she recapped the tube. "Better. Much better." She straightened her shoulders, gave her hair a final pat and whirled for the door to the hall, pausing only to grab her small beaded evening clutch from the end of the bed.

When Jenny emerged from the hall, Nick was standing by the table, looking absolutely splendid in a tux. Something tightened in her chest when she spotted him. In spite of her extreme nervousness, she identified the emotion: pride. She was *proud* to be his date.

Right then, he turned and saw her. The two girls and her mother, at the table, did the same.

There was a moment of echoing silence that made Jenny's ears ring.

Then Nick whistled—a real, bona fide wolf whistle. "Well," he said. "Wow."

In the space of an instant, Jenny's hands stopped shaking and her heart settled down to a nice, easy rhythm. "Why thank you, Nicolas." She let her lashes sweep down modestly. "I'll take that as a compliment."

"Mother." Polly's voice held a note of accusation. "Where did you get that dress?"

"At a department store, I'd imagine," Kirsten said

dryly. She smiled at Jenny. "You look absolutely lovely, Jennifer."

"But you were going to wear that black one," Polly insisted, sounding cheated. "Why didn't you *tell* me you went out and bought something else?"

Jenny felt a bit uncomfortable. Why *hadn't* she mentioned the new dress to her daughter?

Kirsten had a perfectly acceptable answer—even if it wasn't the real one. "Polly Brown, it is not your mother's responsibility to report her every action and decision to you. This is *her* date and, since she is an adult, what she chooses to wear for it is her own concern."

"But Granny, you don't understand. Nick and I—" Polly cut herself off as Nick caught her eye and gave a quick shake of his head. Jenny couldn't decide why he'd done that. Perhaps he only meant that Polly should listen to her grandmother. But maybe he feared she might launch into an explanation of the "training" she was putting him through.

Jenny suspected the latter. Kirsten Lundquist was a no-nonsense sort of woman. She probably wouldn't think too much of her thirteen-year-old granddaughter teaching a grown man how to improve his love life. Nick had always admired Kirsten, so her opinion would matter to him.

"You and Nick *what?*" Kirsten inquired gently.

Polly looked away, brought her hand up to her mouth and surreptitiously tapped at her top row of braces. "Oh, never mind. I guess you're right. It's none of my business."

"You do look really hot, Mrs. Brown," Amelia said

in that sweet, soft voice of hers. Jenny murmured her thanks to the pretty, dark-haired girl.

Polly took her finger out of her mouth and grudgingly added her vote. "Yeah, Mom. You look great."

"And we have to go." Nick cleared the distance between them and put his hand at Jenny's back. Beneath her dress, her skin tingled at his touch. She stiffened, then relaxed. So silly, to be so edgy...

She gave Nick a fond smile, then turned to her mother. "We might be out late."

"Don't you worry. We'll be fine. I'm going to beat these youngsters at this game and then allow them to watch a movie. You two have a terrific time."

A pair of ficus trees woven with twinkle lights flanked the entrance to the huge ballroom. Overhead, recessed corner chandeliers poured a mellow light over the sixty-plus tables set with creamy white china, sparkling glassware and gleaming silverware.

When Nick and Jenny walked in, it looked as if most of the guests had already arrived. The light from the votive candles in the center of each table caught on beaded gowns and diamond earrings. Everywhere Jenny looked, something seemed to be glittering.

They were immediately surrounded by several of Nick's business associates. He greeted them warmly and introduced Jenny. She smiled and said hello and hoped she wouldn't be called upon later to remember all the names.

"You want to get rid of that jacket?" Nick asked, once the crowd around them thinned out a little.

"Good idea." She took it off and handed it over, catching the appreciative light in Nick's eyes as he let his gaze wander over her bare shoulders and downward, to take in the snug, clinging fit of the gown. "Did I tell you I like that dress?"

"I kind of figured you did—when you let out that whistle back at the house."

He winked at her. "Subtle I'm not."

"That's part of your charm."

He disappeared through the crowd. Jenny waited where she was, smiling at people as they moved by her, feeling just a little awkward standing there all alone, but rather enjoying herself nonetheless.

Nick wasn't gone long. "Come on." He tucked her arm in his. "We'd better grab our seats. The waiters are moving in." Jenny glanced out across the acres of tables. Sure enough, men and women in white shirts with black ties were already weaving in and out, serving trays held high.

Nick led Jenny to a table not far from the dance floor, where six of the eight chairs were already filled. The little silver-embossed place cards at the two empty seats read Nick DeSalvo and Guest.

Amidst another flurry of introductions, Nick pulled back Jenny's chair for her. Jenny shook several hands in a row and murmured over and over, "So nice to meet you." It turned out that Nick had built the house of the couple across from them, as well as the offices of the dentist on their left.

Nick said the name of the woman on her right. Jenny stuck out her hand. "So nice to—"

"Jenny. I swear. You don't remember me, do you?"

Jenny blinked—and the woman's name registered. Clarice Hunter. High school. Another honor student, as Jenny herself had been. Andrew and Clarice had dated, before Jenny came along. And Clarice had become…a lawyer, wasn't it?

Clarice knew. About what had happened to Andrew. Jenny could see it in those hazel eyes. The story had made the front page of the *Bee:* ''Man Shot Dead in Doughnut Shop Holdup.'' And, now that Jenny thought about it, she remembered that Clarice had sent flowers to the funeral. A beautiful bouquet of white roses and red carnations.

Jenny felt slightly foolish, not to have remembered her high school rival right away. Foolish and a bit unnerved, to run into Clarice here, among all these strangers, after so many years.

She forged on gamely, ''Clarice. Of course I remember you.''

''How *are* you?''

''I'm…good. I'm just fine.''

''You look terrific.''

''Well, thank you. And how have *you* been?''

Clarice laughed. ''Working. A total career woman, that's me. You're a teacher, right?''

''Yes. Fourth grade.''

''And I seem to recall that you have a little girl…?''

Nick laughed then. ''Not so little anymore. Polly's thirteen now.''

Jenny added, ''She's growing up fast.''

Clarice nodded. ''What's that old joke? Why don't teenagers move out on their own—while they still know it all?''

Jenny let out an obligatory chuckle. ''Well, there is truth in that. Sometimes Polly does drive me nuts. But what can I say? She's bright and beautiful and I adore her.''

"Spoken like the wonderful mother I'm sure you are."

Clarice really did sound sincere. Jenny allowed herself to relax a little. As each second ticked by, it seemed less and less likely that Clarice would start gushing over how sorry she was for Jenny's loss, or that she'd toss out some brittle remark about how Jenny had once stolen Andrew from her. High school, after all, had been a long time ago. And as the years went by since Andrew's death, casual acquaintances tended to be more willing to let the grim subject lie.

The man to Clarice's right, apparently her date, whispered something in her ear. Clarice turned and answered him as a waiter slipped a salad in front of Jenny. Jenny picked up her fork, grateful to have something to put in her mouth that would keep her from having to say 'Nice to meet you' one more time.

Nick leaned close and asked, "Want some dressing on that?" He had picked up the silver condiment server.

"Thank you." She took the server from him and spooned oil and vinegar over the attractive mixture of greens.

"Bread?"

She turned back to him. His dark eyes gleamed at her.

And the strangest thing happened. Some sort of charged impulse seemed to zip around in the air between them. She had a feeling of strong complicity with him, as if they shared a naughty, delicious secret. At the same time, Jenny experienced a lovely, effervescent, lifting sensation, one that alarmed her a little. In recent years, she had often felt close to Nick. But there was something else in this moment now. Something…exciting. Something dangerous. Something that made her feel giddy and way, way too young.

Jenny took a dinner roll and told herself not to let her imagination run away with her.

In the center of the table stood several opened bottles of wine. Nick knew her preferences. He picked up the Chenin Blanc and held it so that she could read the label. She nodded in acceptance and he filled her glass.

Jenny spotted a waiter, serving cocktails from a tray at the next table over. She put her hand on Nick's dark sleeve. He leaned close again and she advised, "Better catch him if you want your Scotch on the rocks."

He nodded and signaled the waiter. A few minutes later, his own drink arrived.

After the main course came a few speeches. The waiters were serving a dessert of caramel mousse when the band started playing. Nick pulled Jenny out onto the dance floor. As he took her in his arms, she found herself trying to remember how long it had been since they had last danced together. Five or six years, at least. And then, it had only happened a few times— back when she and Andrew double-dated with him and someone else. Andrew never cared much for dancing, but Jenny loved it. And so did Nick.

Inevitably, on those double dates, Andrew would end up turning to his friend. "Come on, Nick. Do me a favor. Get Jenny out on that floor where we all know she's dying to be."

And Nick would hold out his hand to her, since his friend had asked him to. Jenny would go out on the floor with him—to please Andrew, she would always tell herself. But the truth was, she really did want to dance. And inevitably, she would forget how much Nick irritated her the minute he started whirling her around the floor.

Now, the first number faded off and the second one started. Nick and Jenny paused, swaying, until Nick picked up the beat again.

Nick asked, "Having fun?"

"Mmm-hmm."

"Me, too. Thanks for saying you'd come."

"My pleasure."

They danced on, pausing and then starting again each time the song changed. Then, as the bandleader announced a short break, a business associate tapped Nick on the shoulder and asked for a few minutes of his time. Nick walked Jenny back to the table. "I won't be long, I promise."

"Don't rush. I'll be fine."

Clarice Hunter sat in her chair alone, sipping red wine. Jenny slid in next to her and poured herself another glass from the bottle of Chenin Blanc.

"A pretty nice party, considering," Clarice said. Jenny set the bottle down and picked up her glass, wondering what that meant. Clarice elaborated, "Oh, you know. Big charity events. The food's usually terrible and the speeches never end."

Jenny sipped. "I guess we all got lucky this time around."

Clarice rested her elbows on the table and ran a slender, beautifully manicured forefinger around the rim of her glass. "You and Nick look good together."

Jenny stared at Clarice for a moment as the implication sank in. And then a laugh of pure surprise escaped her. "You've got it wrong. Nick and I are friends. Very close friends, the past few years—but that's all."

Clarice kept running her finger around and around. "Oh, come on."

Let her think what she wants to think, a voice inside Jenny's head advised. But somehow, she couldn't stop herself from arguing, "No. Seriously. Nick's been wonderful to me and my daughter, since Andrew died. And tonight, well, he needed a date. I said I'd help him out, that's all."

Clarice picked up her glass. "Hmm." She sipped and set the glass down. "I have to tell you, I've been sitting here watching you two dance, wondering why some girls have all the luck."

Jenny thought of Andrew, of the tender, playful way he had kissed her that last time, before he went out the door after jelly-filled doughnuts and never came back. She gave Clarice a level look. "I haven't had all the luck, Clarice. Not by a long shot."

Clarice was the one to drop her gaze. "Yes. Of course. I realize that."

Right then, it occurred to Jenny that maybe something else was going on here. "Are you...interested in Nick?"

Clarice waved one of those slender hands. "What smart single woman in Sacramento isn't? He's a major success story, our Nick DeSalvo."

"Clarice. You know what I mean."

Clarice was silent for a moment, then she answered, "There's nothing. Not really." She shrugged. "A couple of years ago, my firm moved its offices to an older building right here in the downtown area. The whole place had to be gutted, a complete remodel. We hired Nick's construction company to do the job. Nick and I went out to lunch during that time—twice. It never got beyond that. He never even made a pass at me." She sipped more wine. "Darn it."

"So then. You *are* interested in him."

"Jenny." Clarice shook her head. "The point is, the interest has to be mutual."

Jenny made a sympathetic noise and said no more. She'd probably carried the subject too far, anyway.

The band started up again. Clarice spotted her date coming toward them across the dance floor. She stood and brushed out her slim-fitting velvet skirt. "Time to dance. Take care, Jenny."

"You, too." Jenny watched Clarice walk away. Then she glanced around for Nick, but didn't see him. Still off somewhere talking business, no doubt. She had time for a quick trip to the ladies' room.

As she smoothed her hair and freshened her lipstick, Jenny couldn't stop going over the things Clarice had said. Strange. Clarice just wouldn't give up the idea that there was something romantic going on between her and Nick.

And Jenny had to admit that there might be some slight cause for Clarice's suspicions. Jenny and Nick did get along well together these days. And they both liked to dance.

However, if Clarice only knew about Sasha—which Jenny hadn't told her, because Sasha was Nick's business—if Clarice only knew about Sasha, she'd see the whole situation in a different light. She'd understand why Nick hadn't wanted to take a real date to this event tonight. She'd realize that she was way off base about the whole thing.

Jenny found she was glaring at her own reflection in the mirror. She made herself smile, capped her lipstick, gave her hair a final pat and returned to the ballroom once more.

Nick stood by their table, waiting for her. "You disappeared."

"A little nose powdering was in order, that's all."

"Come on, let's dance some more."

He led her out to the floor again and took her in his arms. It was wonderful. Such fun, to be dancing. They never sat down through that whole set, or the one that followed.

By then, it was after midnight. Many of the guests had already left. The waiters hovered against the mauve-colored walls, eager to clean up and go home.

Nick got Jenny's jacket for her and helped her slide her arms into the narrow sleeves. Then they left the ficus trees and twinkle lights behind. Outside, the parking valet fetched Nick's Cadillac. He held open Jenny's door and she settled herself into the soft leather seat.

They were driving past Capitol Park when Nick asked her if she'd like to stop somewhere for one last drink.

The idea pleased her. She started to say yes, but then she glanced over at him and it occurred to her that stopping for one last drink was just a little too much like something lovers might do. "I really ought to get home, I think."

He shrugged. "All right. If you have to."

"I do. Really."

"Fine. I'll take you on home."

She said no more and neither did he. The powerful car hummed through the dark streets. Jenny started to feel a little sad. A little...forlorn.

She'd had such a lovely time. And now it was over. Nick would drop her off at her door. She'd go in. Say good night to Polly and Amelia and her mother, if they were still up. She might have to field a few nosy questions from Polly. Then she'd go down the hall to her room, take off the beautiful dress, hang it in her closet—back there with the black one she hadn't worn in over four years. How long would it be until she might wear a dress like it again?

The answer came, as sad and forlorn as she felt right then: probably a long time. Maybe she'd never wear such a dress again.

Soon enough, Nick pulled into her driveway next to her mother's big blue Buick. He got out and came around to open her door—but she'd already pushed it wide. He reached for her hand.

Some contrary mood had hold of her. She pretended not to notice his gentlemanly gesture and rose without his aid. He stepped back, out of her way, and closed the door behind her. Jenny hurried around the front of the two cars, headed for her own front door.

A greenish light bled through the blinds over the kitchen window. Jenny knew what that meant. The girls were watching a movie in the family room, with all the rest of the lights off. Behind her, Nick stepped up onto the porch.

Jenny grabbed the doorknob.

It was locked. Nick waited, at her back, way too

close, it seemed to her. She could feel the warmth of him—and his size and strength.

"Jen?"

She didn't want to turn, to look at him. All at once, she felt cornered. In danger—though Nick would never in the world do her harm.

She flipped the clasp on her beaded bag and felt in there for the key.

"Jen?"

Her hand closed on the cool metal. She pulled it out of the bag—and dropped it.

With a small noise of frustration, she bent down to grab for it. Nick did the same. He got there before she did and retrieved the key.

They both stood, ended up once again with her facing the door and Nick right at her back.

"Jen?" She felt his breath, he was so close. It tickled the feathery hairs at her nape.

She thought of that charged moment at the banquet, when he had looked at her and she had felt as if they shared some exciting, rather naughty secret.

And she thought of what Clarice Hunter had said. *Some girls have all the luck...He never even made a pass at me...*

Nick had never made a pass at Jenny, either.

But she had the most alarming suspicion that he intended to.

Right now.

Chapter Five

"Jen." She felt the caress of his breath again, warm and sweet along her ear.

She knew she couldn't just stand there forever, facing away from him, refusing to answer him.

"Jen, are you all right?"

She made herself turn. She looked into his eyes.

She saw affection. And concern.

And nothing else, really.

He took her hand, which suddenly felt small and icy; his was so big and warm. He dropped the key into her palm. And he smiled. "You seem mad all of a sudden. What's the matter?"

She had to fully admit it to herself, then. Nick had no intention of making a pass at her, no intention at all.

Conflicting emotions roiled inside her. Embarrassment. Relief. Totally uncalled-for irritation at him.

His dark brows drew together. "Something *is* wrong. What?"

She gulped. "No, really. It's nothing." Except her own foolish and presumptuous imagination. He was Nick and he was her friend and she ought to be ashamed of herself for imagining that he would suddenly decide to put a move on her. He had *never* made a pass at her. Never. Not in the years they'd only tolerated each other for Andrew's sake. And not in the years since they had become true friends.

"Jen?"

She commanded herself to stop pondering her own foolishness and give the poor man a reply. "Oh, Nick. Of course I'm not mad."

He still looked a little apprehensive. "Are you *sure* there's not something?"

"Positive. Except maybe that I hate for the evening to end."

That pleased him. She watched his face relax, saw a smile take form. "Whew." He was still holding her hand. He gave it a squeeze. "You had me worried there."

"Well, stop it. I had a great time. Do you want to come in?"

He seemed to consider, then shook his head and released her hand. "Naw. Better not. It's getting kind of late."

"Yes. I suppose so."

He started walking backward, down the single step, then along the walk toward his waiting car, grinning all the way. Finally, with a quick salute, he turned and disappeared behind the wall of the garage. Jenny stood there beneath the porch light, waiting, until he started the car, pulled out into the street and waved at her as he drove away.

Inside, the girls sat on the floor of the family room, with a bowl of popcorn between them and a can of Dr. Pepper each. They were watching a black-and-white horror movie. Jenny came up behind them and stopped just a few feet away. On the screen, a hideous, wild-haired woman in a tattered nightgown pulled a cockroach off a tree and shoved it into her mouth, then chewed with ghoulish gusto. The scene cut to an interior, where a pretty blonde clutched the sides of her face and screamed in fright—not too loudly, thank goodness; the girls had remembered to keep the sound low.

Jenny looked down at the two of them, realizing that she'd expected Polly to be waiting at the front door, eager to hear everything about the evening in order to gather more background for her training sessions with Nick. Instead, in true thirteen-year-old fashion, Polly and her friend had found a movie to watch and Polly had forgotten all about her mother and Nick and their big date.

The girls stared at the screen as if in a mutual trance. Jenny doubted they even knew she was there.

But then, without taking her eyes from the grisly scenes before her, Polly muttered, "Hi, Mom," and Amelia raised her hand in a vague sort of half wave, then went ahead and completed the gesture by feeling for the popcorn bowl and scooping up a handful of the fluffy white kernels. Of course, Polly wouldn't have any. She wasn't allowed to, with her braces.

"Having fun?" Jenny asked.

In unison, the girls said, "Mmm-hmm," never

blinking, never shifting their eyes from the flickering screen, where a large group of ghoulish types now staggered through the darkness toward a run-down clapboard house. Amelia shoved popcorn into her mouth and chewed as she watched.

"Granny's gone on to bed, I take it."

"Mmm-hmm."

"Well. I guess I'll turn in, too."

"'Night, Mom."

"'Night, Mrs. Brown."

Jenny turned for the hall, then couldn't resist a motherly admonition. "As soon as that one's over, turn it off and go to bed."

"We will…"

"Okay…"

In her room, Jenny took off her beautiful dress, put it carefully away and then changed to her flannelette pajamas. She cleaned her teeth and washed her face. In bed, with the lights off, she wondered if she'd ever get to sleep. She kept thinking of the night just passed, of herself and Nick. Dancing.

Of her foolishness at the front door, when she'd let herself imagine that he intended to kiss her.

Of Clarice Hunter, who wished Nick wanted her.

Of the mysterious Sasha Overfield, whom Nick *did* want, but who apparently didn't want him back.

Of how truly confusing and frustrating male-female relationships could be.

When dawn came, she was still lying there, staring at nothing, telling herself to relax and go to sleep.

Monday night, Nick and Polly argued about *Wuthering Heights* all through dinner. Nick thought that *both* Heathcliffe and Cathy were "a couple of pig-headed fools, who *should* have gotten married to each other, because they *deserved* each other."

When he made that announcement, Polly dropped her fork to her plate, tossed her head and let out a great sigh. "Nick. On the deepest level, *Wuthering Heights* isn't really even about a man named Heathcliffe and a woman called Cathy. On the deepest level, it's about the man and the woman in *all* of us, the male and female forces, which battle each other constantly, but which must be reconciled, if we ever hope to have a prayer for happiness."

At that point, Nick grunted in thoroughly masculine disgust. "Look. Who wants to read a book about people like that? She's a spoiled brat and he's got a chip the size of a backhoe on his shoulder. Somebody should have given her a spanking—and he should have gone ahead and bumped himself off when she died and saved everyone else in the damn book a half a lifetime of suffering." He sawed off a bite of pot roast and stuck it into his mouth.

"Cathy is a passionate person, Nick. And Heathcliffe has been through a living hell."

"Cathy is a spoiled twit. And lots of people go through hell. Not all of them decide to systematically wreck the lives of everyone else in sight." Nick cut more meat. "All I'm saying is, give me someone I can root for, at least." He winked at Jenny. "This is one terrific pot roast, Jen."

She gave him a smile.

Polly huffed, "Someone you can *root* for? This isn't entertainment reading you're doing here, Nick."

"Oh, hey. I got that. And, now you mention it,

maybe we ought to stick to the self-help articles and the romantic movies on video. The poems and the hundred-year-old English novels are just plain over my head.''

"They are not. You have to work a little to understand them, that's all.''

"Yeah, and I work all day long. I don't need to be up all night trying to plow through some book about two people I don't even like.''

Polly's face was flushed. She argued with real fervor, "But you said that Sasha was a *reader*. I'm sure she's read the books and poems we've been discussing. It's important that you read and understand them, too. That way, when you get back together again, you'll be able to talk about the things that matter to her.''

Nick impaled a carrot on his fork, paused with it halfway to his mouth—and allowed that, okay, maybe Polly was right.

"Of course I'm right." And she launched into further elucidations of the deeper meanings of the novel in question.

Naturally Nick took issue with just about every point she made. Jenny quietly ate her own pot roast and vegetables and then got up and carried her plate to the sink. Still arguing, Nick and Polly cleared off the rest of the meal and continued the discussion in the kitchen, as the three of them worked like the cleanup team they'd somehow become to rinse the dishes, load the dishwasher and wash and dry the pots and pans.

Jenny left them to their debate. She had a few math

fact study sheets to draw up and the usual stack of papers to correct.

But when she sat down at her desk, she found herself alternately doodling on her deskpad and staring off into space—not getting down to what needed doing at all.

She could hear the murmur of voices in the main part of the house. Nick and Polly, still going at it. She smiled. In spite of the contentious nature of all of their discussions, Jenny knew that both of them were having a great time.

Just as she had, on Saturday night.

Jenny's smile faded to a frown.

She kept thinking of Saturday night. Of how much fun it had been. Of the way they had danced. How much they had laughed.

Also since Saturday, she kept thinking about other things. Things she had no business pondering.

For instance, how handsome Nick seemed lately.

More handsome than before—though Jenny had always thought of him as a good-looking man. Maybe a little too overwhelmingly *male*. A complete guy's guy, with that devilish smile of his, his tendency toward wolf whistles, his preference for a cold one in a can over a nice glass of white wine.

Yes, a complete guy's guy. And too handsome by half. Tonight, when he had come up the front walk, Jenny had been turning from the stove. She'd glanced out the kitchen window and spotted him, strolling toward the front door, wearing good slacks and a dress shirt, his jacket slung over his shoulder, probably fresh from some meeting or other concerning one of his current projects.

Her heart had actually lurched inside her chest—and then started beating way, way too fast. She'd thought, Oh my, there he is: Nick!

Such reactions were extremely unnerving.

And a little bit embarrassing.

Why, Saturday night, after the party, as she was lying there in bed unable to sleep, she had really gone too far.

Her mind had kept circling the events of the evening, around thoughts of Nick and the things that Clarice Hunter had said. Around the subject of Sasha Overfield and the baffling nature of male-female relationships.

As dawn had crept up on her, she had actually let herself wonder about that little remark Nick had made when he showed up on her doorstep at two a.m. on the anniversary of Andrew's death. That remark about the "hot sex" he and Sasha had shared.

She knew Nick pretty well, after all. And she had met a number of his girlfriends over the years. He'd always preferred the offbeat when it came to women: artists and musicians, women who went their own way and made their own rules, women who tended to have interests totally separate from his own. There'd been that flugel player and that performance artist. Also, he'd dated a lady biker and a woman who directed some underground theater group downtown. They'd all seemed just as ill-suited to him in the long run as Sasha probably was.

But the long run, until now, had never been Nick's concern. He'd honestly admitted that he just wanted a good time—a few drinks and a few laughs. Nick had always worked hard, building his construction business and then expanding into property development. He wanted someone to party with at the end of a hard working week.

And Jenny had no doubt he'd gotten just that.

Really, there had always been a certain aura, between Nick and whatever woman he was seeing at any given moment. An atmosphere that could only be called sexual. Nick's women always looked at him with shining, dreamy eyes. They looked extremely *satisfied,* those women. As if they were getting just what they wanted, and plenty of it, too.

As she lay there, thinking about Nick's old girlfriends and the hot sex they must have enjoyed with him, Jenny had actually let herself wonder about what it might be like to have a little hot sex with Nick herself. To feel his big, warm hands on her skin, to turn into his arms and have it be more than dancing they were doing. To have him there, under the covers with her, kissing her and caressing her. Pulling her against his big, powerful body. Making her sigh and moan...

Now, at her desk in the spare room, Jenny shut her eyes and put her head down on the blank sheet of paper that should, by then, have been filled with times tables in her neatly rounded schoolteacher's hand. Her face burned with mortification.

Oh, there was no excuse for thoughts like that. No excuse at all.

Jenny lifted her head and stared rather blankly at the little cubbyholes and shelves in the top half of her desk. Right then, out in the other room, Nick laughed—a deep, rumbling, very masculine sound. A warm, delicious shiver started at Jenny's solar plexus and moved outward, along her arms and her legs, just beneath the surface of her skin, to the very tips of her toes and the ends of each finger.

Out in the other room, Nick laughed again.

Jenny rose from her desk, rushed across the room and shut the door—carefully, so neither Nick nor Polly would hear her do it.

There. Now she could hardly hear him at all. She returned to her desk, sat down again—and felt like a total fool.

Honestly. Closing the door just to keep his *voice* from reaching her.

Pitiful. That's what it was.

Maybe she needed to get out more. Maybe Saturday night—and Nick himself—had assumed so much importance suddenly because she never went out. Maybe having Nick underfoot all the time, the way he seemed to be lately, made her focus too much on the lack of a man in her life.

She hadn't dated at all since Andrew had died. She'd seen no reason to. She had Polly and her students. And once the stunning pain of her grief had faded a little, her daughter and her work had always seemed like enough. No other man could ever take Andrew's place. She'd come to accept that, felt quite comfortable with it.

Until just recently.

But now that she really started giving the whole issue some thought, maybe enjoying a man's company every once in a while would be a good thing for her. She'd had a few offers of dinner and a show. What harm could it do to say yes when the next offer came her way?

She wouldn't have to get married again, or become

intimate with anyone. She could just…have a nice time. Enjoy adult conversation and a little companionship.

There was certainly nothing at all wrong with that.

In fact, only last week, Roger Bayliss, who taught fifth grade at her school, had asked her if she'd seen the latest Jack Nicholson film. She'd murmured something vague about waiting for it to come out on video, and left it at that.

But now that she thought about it, Roger did seem to like her. He'd been divorced from his wife, Sally, for a little over a year now. And in the past few months, he always seemed to end up sitting next to her in the teacher's lounge, during breaks. He would joke with her and pay her compliments—and drop hints that sometime they ought to get together for dinner or something.

He also knew all about what had happened to Andrew. He'd been kind and supportive during that awful time right afterward, just like everyone else at her school. They were friends, she and Roger, in the casual way that colleagues often are. Dating him wouldn't be like going out with a stranger. They shared the common ground of their work, and a basic knowledge of each other's lives.

Nick laughed again, in the other room. Even through the closed door, Jenny could hear it: deep and rich and full. Her whole body suddenly felt heavy and weak. Her breathing changed, grew shallow and slow….

Ridiculous.

Before she could think of a reason to stop herself, Jenny bent and picked up her briefcase. In it, she kept a photocopied list of the phone numbers and addresses of everyone who worked at her school.

Roger Bayliss was the second name on the list. She picked up the phone and punched up the numbers—quickly, with authority, as if she knew what she was doing, as if she called a man and asked him out every other day.

It rang twice, and then she heard his voice. "This is Roger."

"Hi. It's Jenny. Jenny Brown?"

"Jenny? Well. Hello, there." He sounded really pleased.

"Yes. Hello."

A silence. He was waiting for her to say why she'd called. She made herself begin. "I...well, I was just thinking. About that Jack Nicholson movie you mentioned last week? Um, you see, I was wondering if maybe..." Oh, she was making a mess of it. She gulped in a breath and sent the words out in a rush. "Roger, tell me, what are you doing this Friday night?"

He laughed. Not as deep or rich a laugh as Nick's laugh, but a fine laugh. A very *nice* laugh. "Jenny. I don't believe it. I think you're asking me out."

She didn't let herself waver. "I am, Roger. I'm asking you out for Friday night. To go to that Jack Nicholson movie you mentioned. What do you say?"

"I say yes, Jenny Brown. I'd like that very much."

As soon as she hung up, unreality assailed Jenny.

She couldn't believe it. She'd called a man and asked him on a date.

Once again, she sat for several minutes, just staring at the cubbyholes in the top of her desk. Maybe it hadn't been a very good idea. Maybe she shouldn't have done it.

But she had. And she would go through with it. Yes, she would.

She would go out with Roger Bayliss on Friday night.

And she would have a lovely time.

And just maybe the experience would help her to get all those obsessive thoughts of last Saturday night—and her dear friend, Nick—out of her mind.

She picked up the phone again and gave her mother a call. Kirsten said she'd be glad to come over on Friday and keep Polly company, then she added, "Though I really do think Polly's getting old enough to stay home alone."

"I know," Jenny told her, idly swiveling her chair around away from her desk. "I think the time's coming. Very soon now."

"But not quite yet?"

Jenny agreed, "Not quite yet."

Kirsten chuckled. "You're so protective."

Jenny frowned at the phone. "Too protective, you mean?"

"Oh, maybe a little. But it's all right. Being too protective is certainly better than not protective enough—and I do like to see you getting out a little. Is this…someone special?"

Jenny thought of Roger, of his friendly smile and his pleasant laugh. "No, not really. He's nice, though."

"I'm sure you'll have a lovely time."

"Yes. Me, too." Jenny stared at the door she'd shut,

thinking again of Nick on the other side of it, of last Saturday night....

Her mother asked, "Should I bring those two felt boards you wanted to use in your class when I come on Friday, then?"

Jenny went on staring at the door, seeing Nick in her mind, the way his dark eyes could shine, the threads of silver in his black hair, the muscular breadth of his shoulders, the strength in his big hands....

"Jennifer? The felt boards?"

Jenny closed her eyes, let out a breath and turned back to her desk. "You know, I planned to use them on Friday, so Friday night will be too late. Could I drop by before then and pick them up?"

Kirsten said she'd have them ready.

A few minutes later, Jenny said goodbye to her mother. Then she took pen in hand and resolutely concentrated on getting those math fact sheets done. By the time she finished them and the stack of papers that needed grading, Nick had gone for the night.

Chapter Six

On Tuesday, Nick reached Jenny's house at his usual time, his favorite time—about dinnertime. He parked in the driveway and started up the walk, his hands stuffed in his pockets to ward off the evening chill. Overhead, the sky was clear, the stars growing brighter as the night came on. A pale, almost-full moon hovered above the budding branches of the huge old mulberry tree in the middle of Jenny's lawn.

He was almost to the front step when he heard the rustling sound. Nick paused on the walk and peered through the gathering gloom at the bed of big-leaf ivy that grew close to the house.

There. He saw it. A ball of orange fuzz. Orange fuzz with wide golden eyes, peeking out at him from under the canopy of large, heart-shaped leaves.

A damn kitten.

"Rreow?" It was a tiny, pitiful sound from a puny-looking animal. Right then, a little orange head, topped by a pair of pointy ears, rose above the tangle of leaves. *"Rreow?"* it asked again.

Nick stomped his boot on the walk, thinking to chase it away, back to wherever it belonged. "Git. Scoot."

The kitten didn't scoot. The orange head dipped back beneath the ivy, but that was all. Those golden eyes, gone even wider, kept right on looking at him.

With a shrug, Nick turned from those eyes and went up the step to the front door.

Warm light spilled out from between the open blinds of the kitchen window. He could see Jenny in there, the brightness catching on her pale blond hair, making it gleam. She saw him, too, and smiled.

The door was open so he went in, the warmth and the mouthwatering smells of Jenny's house at dinnertime enveloping him. He went straight to the kitchen and leaned in the doorway.

Jen was tearing lettuce into a big wooden bowl. She glanced over her shoulder and smiled at him again. "Hey."

"Hey. Where's Polly?"

"On the phone with Amelia." Jenny rinsed a big red tomato and shook it dry. "They're making plans for this Saturday night."

"Plans?"

She turned toward him, still holding the tomato. "Amelia's been invited to a party, by some kids from her new school over there in Greenhaven. There will actually be *boys* at that party."

"Whoa. Boys. Scary."

"Right. Amelia asked Polly to go, too—and then to stay overnight. They're working out all the details. The really important stuff. Like what to wear."

"Working out the details. That could take a while, right?"

"Exactly." Jenny's expression said it all. It was a mother's expression, patient and knowing, affectionate and amused. "You may end up setting the table all by yourself."

"I think I can handle it. I'll do anything for a free meal."

"I noticed." She grinned, then turned back to her work, picking up a knife and starting in on that tomato, cutting it in wedges.

Nick lingered there, in the open entrance from the dining room, watching her, thinking that when he married Sasha it would be just like this every evening. He'd come home and the house would smell like dinner. He'd lean in the kitchen doorway, watching as she cut up the salad. And he would feel just generally terrific about the world and his place in it.

A home. Like this one. That was what he wanted. A place to come to, with the right woman in it, a place that gave meaning to a hard day of checking up on contractors and arguing over record drawings.

Funny how it could take some guys almost half a lifetime to figure out something so simple, while other guys—guys like Andy—knew it from the first.

Andy. Nick shook his head. Still, even after four years, he felt a certain tightness across his chest when Andy came to mind. The tall, skinny kid with the chemistry book under one arm and the basketball in the other had been the best kind of friend. Someone a guy could talk to. About anything. Someone who had a lot of stuff figured out early, but would never rub your face in what he knew.

The truth was, Nick still talked to Andy. Not that he would admit such a thing to anyone else. People would think he was a few cans short of a six-pack, if they knew. So Nick kept his mouth shut about it. The way he saw it, his little talks with Andy did him a hell of a lot of good. And they were nobody's business but his own.

Jenny pulled a mushroom from a plastic bag, rinsed it quickly, wiped the water off with a paper towel and went to work on it with her knife.

Nick wondered, was Sasha cooking dinner right now?

He'd never actually seen Sasha cook anything. In the short time they were together, they'd always eaten out. But she wanted a husband, just as he wanted a wife. And maybe it didn't matter who did the cooking, as long as it got done. He could cook a little himself, as a matter of fact. The important thing was that they sat down together, as he did now almost every night, with Jen and Polly. The sitting down together, passing the food around, gave a real feeling of completeness to the day.

Jenny was slicing green onions now. She glanced at him again, a questioning kind of look, as if she didn't know what he was up to, just standing there, watching her.

He thought of the little ball of fur, crouched out there in the ivy. "Any of your neighbors got a kitten? A scroungy-looking orange one?"

She set the knife aside, gathered up the sliced onions

in both hands and dropped them into the bowl. Then she rinsed her hands and reached for a towel. "A kitten?" She wiped her hands dry. "Not that I know of. Why?"

"There's one out in the ivy, under the living-room window."

"You're kidding."

"Nope."

Jenny hung up the towel. "Show me."

He led her out the way he'd come, pulling open the front door and gesturing her through ahead of him. They went down the single step to the walk and he pointed at the spot in the ivy, where he'd seen the kitten. "It was right there, all curled up under the leaves. It stuck out its head and meowed at me."

Jenny peered where he pointed. "I suppose it's wandered off. Maybe back wherever it came from."

Right then, behind them, the front door opened and Polly demanded, "What's going on, you guys?"

Jen said, "Nick saw a kitten out here. But it looks like it's gone now."

"A kitten?" Polly's green eyes started gleaming. She might be thirteen and always claiming how grown-up she was, but the thought of a kitten turned her into a real kid again. Slamming the door behind her, she hurried to join them at the edge of the walk. "How big was it? What color was it? Where did you say you saw it?" Not waiting for any answers, she moved out onto the lawn. "Here kitty, kitty, kitty, kitty," she sang out in that high, nerve-slicing voice all females seemed to use instinctively when it came to calling cats.

She got halfway to the edge of the house when the kitten answered, *"Rreow?"*

"Come on, come on, kitty, kitty, kitty…"

Ivy rustled. They watched the leaves move, as the animal came around the corner of the house, headed straight for Polly.

"Kitty, kitty, kitty…"

The orange ball of fur popped out at Polly's feet and sat down, those pointy ears straight up. *"Rreow?"*

"Oh, you little sweetie. Oh, you darling thing…" Polly knelt and scooped the kitten into her arms. "Oh, just look at her." Polly rose to her feet and turned to face Nick and Jen. "Isn't she the most adorable little sweetheart of a cat?" The kitten, clearly no fool when it came to grabbing its chance, rubbed its pointy-eared head against Polly's stroking hand. Polly glanced up. Her eyes found Jen. "Mom. Look at her. She doesn't even have a collar. It's obvious she really needs a home." Polly cradled the kitten close, as if she'd just yanked it from the jaws of death.

Jen looked pained. "Polly…"

Polly started bargaining. "I'll take care of her. I *promise*. I'll do everything she needs. I'll be the one who feeds her. And the litter box—I can handle that, too. You won't have to do a thing, Mom, I swear you won't. I'll be responsible for everything…"

"Honey, she probably belongs to one of the neighbors."

"She doesn't. She's *homeless*. I know it. Her fur's all matted. Nobody loves her. The poor little thing."

Jen sighed. "Well, come on. It's cold out here. Let's go in the house to talk about this."

Polly nuzzled the kitten. "She'll have to come in,

too. We can't just leave her out here, in the cold and the dark, for some big dog to eat."

Nick smiled to himself. Polly had once owned both a big gray cat and a little, yippy brown dog. Andy had got them for her, a few days after they moved into this house. But the cat had gone to that big scratching post in the sky a couple of years ago and the dog had died not long after. No doubt Jen had let herself imagine that Polly's pet-owning days were through.

No such luck. Polly was looking very noble. "Mom. You know I'm right. We cannot just leave a poor, defenseless animal out here in the cold."

Jen glanced at Nick, a what-can-I-do kind of look. Nick lifted an eyebrow at her. He understood her dilemma. He'd seen how Polly operated with Jen sometimes. The kid could be downright relentless. And Jen too often gave in to her. And then there was the damn kitten. Cute. Pitiful. Just the kind of thing Jen couldn't turn away, even if all of Polly's big promises to take care of the animal would be forgotten in a week.

"Mom..." Polly pleaded, using only the one word. *"Mom..."*

Jen sighed again. "Oh, all right. Bring the kitten with you."

Polly grinned hugely for once, showing the braces she usually tried to hide. And then she hurried to join them. Jen went through the front door first. Nick hung back to let Polly go through before him. That way he could close the door and it wouldn't get slammed.

Polly headed straight for the kitchen.

Jen stopped her. "Hold it. Where are you going?"

"The kitchen, where the light is nice and bright, so I can look her over and see if she's hurt or anything."

"On the *floor*," Jen said. "Not on my counters."

"Oh, all right. Can you get me a towel or something *comfortable* to put her on, at least."

The three of them ended up crouched on the kitchen floor around the kitten, which Polly put down carefully on the towel Jen brought her from one of the hall cabinets.

"She *is* pretty dirty," Jen said. The orange fur looked grimy in the bright light, and dark trails ran down from the big golden eyes.

"But she doesn't seem to have fleas." Polly pushed her fingers through the orange fur, pulling the hair aside enough to see the skin in spots.

Nick couldn't resist teasing a little, "You keep calling it a she? How do you *know* it's a she?"

Polly sent a really snooty look his way. And then she laid the kitten on its back and checked in the right spot. She looked up in triumph. "It's a female. So there."

"You're sure?"

"Nick. I am not an idiot. I know the difference between a male and a female."

Jen had to get into it then. "All right. Let me see." She bent down and had a look for herself. By then, the cat was getting pretty tired of being on its back. It started squirming. Jen said, "All right. Let her up."

Polly grinned, a smug, tight grin, with her lips together. It was an expression she put on pretty often, since she could do it without showing any metal. "See. I'm right." She lifted the kitten into her arms again and rubbed her cheek against the small, fuzzy head. "She's a girl. And I've checked her over good. She's not going to give us any diseases, I'm sure of it."

Jen made a low sound in her throat. "Polly, you are hardly a veterinarian."

"Then we'll *take* her to a veterinarian. And see what he says."

"No, what we will do is call a few of the neighbors and ask if they've lost a cat. In fact, *you* can do that. Right now. While Nick sets the table for dinner."

Polly made seven or eight phone calls. None of the neighbors she talked to knew anything about a lost cat.

"We'll keep asking around," Jenny said. She was definitely feeling trapped. She knew Polly would hit the roof if she suggested that they take the kitten to the animal shelter.

Polly kept up the pressure. "Okay, Mom. We'll keep asking around. But in the meantime, can we keep her? Please. She really needs us, Mom and—"

"Right now, dinner's ready."

"Dinner." Polly looked down at the cat, which she'd hardly let go of since it emerged from the ivy out in the front yard. "That's right. She's probably *starving*. We have to feed her something. You hold her while I get some milk and warm it up a little and then—"

"Polly. Put her in the bathroom. Make a nice little bed for her with that towel and—"

"But she's probably *hungry*. We can't just sit down and eat without feeding her *something*."

Jenny cast a glance at Nick, who had started all this. He was standing over by the table, behind the chair he always sat in now. He saw her look at him and swiftly cut his eyes away, toward the chicken casserole she'd just carried from the oven and set down on a trivet, ready to serve, between the wooden bowl of green salad and the basket of rolls. She felt fondness, and a little stab of irritating attraction—and impatience that he wasn't doing a darn thing to help her out here.

"*Mom.* She must be *hungry,*" Polly insisted again.

"If she eats now, she'll just need to do her business. And we don't even have a litter box."

Polly's eyes widened. "That's right. We've got to get over to a pet shop right away. We've got to—"

"After dinner."

Polly blinked as she registered the implication in her mother's words. "We *can* go, then?"

"I suppose we'll have to."

"Good." Polly thought for a moment, then added, "Mom. I really think we ought to just go now."

"Put her in the bathroom, Polly. Make her as comfortable as you can. And then shut the door."

"But *Mom…*"

"Polly." Nick finally spoke up. "Come on. Let's eat. The quicker we eat, the quicker you'll get to that pet store."

Polly let out a frustrated moan. But she did give in at last—more or less. "She has to have water."

"Fine," Jenny conceded. "Make her comfortable on her towel and fill a cereal bowl with water, close the door so she can't get out—and wash your hands. Now."

The dinner was a rushed affair. Polly shoveled the food in, eager to get on to the next order of business: the trip to the pet store. Periodically, from the bathroom, the little kitten meowed, which only caused Polly to stuff the food in faster. She was up and eager to get going within six minutes of when she sat down.

"Hey." Nick batted her arm away when she tried to snatch his plate. "Back off. I'm not done."

"Nick. We have to get going. We have a lot to do, you know. We've got to get Daisy's things, get her all settled in and comfy and then you and I have to get to work."

He scoffed, *"Daisy?"*

"Yes." Polly sniffed. "I'm going to call her Daisy. I think it's a cute name and it fits her, she's so...sunny-looking."

"Scroungy-looking is what she is."

"She won't be, once I get her cleaned up. And now, eat that if you're going to. We have to leave." She glanced at Jenny. "Mom. I've been thinking."

Uh-oh, Jenny thought, but had the good sense not to say.

Polly continued, "We'd better take Daisy along with us. She'll be just terrified, all alone in a strange bathroom, starving, probably needing to use a litter box, crying out to no one, wondering what will happen to her."

Jenny spoke clearly and slowly. "I am not taking that kitten anywhere in my car tonight."

"We can take Nick's—"

"Stop. No. The kitten stays here."

"Oh, *Mother.*" Polly looked thoroughly miffed. She stuck her nose in the air. "Then I'll just have to stay here, I guess. I simply refuse to leave her alone."

"Fine. Stay here. And don't give her any milk while I'm gone."

"But if she's *hungry...*"

"No milk. First of all, cow's milk is not really that good for a cat."

"But all cats drink—"

"Polly. Stop interrupting me."

Polly glared mutinously—but did keep her mouth shut.

Jenny explained, "Cow's milk isn't that good for cats. And I want her to have a litter box available before we feed her anything. Clear?"

"Sure, Mom. All right."

Nick stood then and picked up his plate. "I'll help Polly clear off the table, and then we can go."

At his offhanded words, a forbidden thrill shivered through Jenny. She pictured the two of them, walking the aisles of the pet store together. Choosing a cat litter, grabbing cans of cat food, picking out a cute little cat bed and a scratching post, while all the while her knees felt weak and her heart beat disconcertingly hard inside her chest.

"No, really, Nick. I can do it myself. It's not a problem at all."

He stopped halfway to the kitchen. "You sure?"

She nodded. "Make yourself useful. Get the dishes cleaned up."

Jenny went to a store called the Pet Emporium. It was as big as a supermarket and open until midnight. A brilliant idea came to her as she was standing at the cat food shelves, trying to choose from about fifty different brands.

This could be good, she thought. This could be...perfect.

As she loaded several cans and a small bag of dry kitten food into her cart, she was smiling to herself.

Yes, this situation with the kitten would work out fine, after all.

At home, Jenny parked in the garage and entered the house through the kitchen. Polly was waiting for her, still holding the kitten, which looked a bit cleaner than when Jenny had left. "I brushed her and washed the gunk out of her eyes," Polly announced. "Did you get the food? And the litter?"

Jenny set down the big bag she'd carried in from the garage with her. "I got everything she'll need. The rest is in the trunk."

"I'll get it," Nick volunteered. He went out and came back with everything else piled in his arms: litter and the cat box and the cute, soft cat bed.

Polly had put the kitten down on the kitchen floor, where it sat quite patiently, waiting, as Polly fumbled in a drawer, looking for the can opener so she could give her a meal.

Nick said, "Where do you want all this?"

And Jenny said, "Actually, while I was at the pet store, I had an idea."

Something in her voice must have alerted the two of them, because they both froze and turned to look at her wearing expressions of distrust.

"What?" said Polly.

"Idea?" asked Nick.

"Yes," Jenny told them cheerfully. "I think Nick is the one who should keep little Daisy."

Chapter Seven

Polly had the can opener in her hand. She plunked it on the counter, hard. "What? *Nick?* Oh, *Mother.*"

Nick chimed in. "Yeah, Jen. That's nuts. The last thing I need is a cat."

But Jenny had it all figured out. "Listen, you two. Think. Here you are, every night, discussing *Wuthering Heights* and How-I-Found-True-Love-And-Kept-It articles from *Woman's Day.* You're supposed to be working to get Nick in touch with the gentler, more sensitive side of himself."

Frowning, Polly bent down. She picked up Daisy, stood again and began rubbing the kitten under its fuzzy chin.

Jenny gestured at the kitten. "And here we have little Daisy, who shows up on our doorstep. Needing love. Needing someone to care for her..."

Nick dropped all the cat paraphernalia on the section of counter at the pass-through to the family room. "Uh-uh. No way. I've got no room in my life for a damn cat. Tell your mother, Pol. Tell her there is no way I can—"

Polly gazed down at the kitten. "You know, maybe Mom's right."

Nick blinked. "Huh?"

Polly met Nick's eyes. She looked a little sad—but determined. "I said, maybe Mom's right."

Nick backed a step toward the door he'd just come through. "Hey. Wait. You *never* think your mother's right. And you want that cat. I can see it. You're *crazy* about that cat."

Polly nodded. "Maybe I am. But you need her more than I do."

"*Need* her? I don't need her. What the hell would I do with her?"

"Love her. Treat her *gently*. Show her how much you care."

Nick actually groaned. "Look. I'm not even home most of the time. She'd spend her whole damn life alone."

Polly tipped her head, considering that. Then she advised, "Well, if she ends up seeming too lonely, we can always go to the animal shelter and pick out a friend to keep her company while you're at work."

Nick scowled. "Great. Then I'll have *two* damn cats I don't need."

Shamelessly, Jenny threw in the argument she'd been saving. "Nick. I seem to recall you mentioning that Sasha loves cats."

"That's right." Polly's eyes lit up. "You said she's got a cat. A cat that she really loves."

"*She* loves it. Not me. I'm no cat-lover. If I had to get a pet, it would be a dog. A big, mean one with lots of sharp teeth."

Polly made a tongue-clucking sound. "Nick. You have to face this. You need Daisy. And Daisy needs you."

"Uh-uh. No way."

Jenny found that she rather enjoyed seeing Nick on the run. "Nick, remember your goal here. You keep saying you want to develop some common ground with Sasha. Learning to love and care for a cat would be a very effective way to do that."

He looked so pathetic as he cast desperately about for more excuses. "Well, I'm reading the books, aren't I? And studying all those magazine articles. And listening to that Enya woman wail on those CDs. Isn't it enough?"

Polly held out the kitten. "Come on. Take her. You're even the one who found her. It makes me kind of sad, because I'd like to have her. But I think she's really meant to be yours."

"*Meant* to be mine? What? Now we're talking about fate here? Making something mystical out of some stray ball of fuzz? I don't think so. Uh-uh. No. Nix. Forget it."

Polly pushed the kitten at him again. "You haven't even *held* her, Nick."

"I don't need to hold her. And *she* doesn't need to be held by *me.*"

"She does, too. Look at her. She's got no one, and you found her. Come on, now. Take your cat."

Nick had backed himself all the way to the door. Polly pushed little Daisy right up against his broad chest—and then let go.

He had to catch her or let her fall to the floor.

With a muttered curse, he made a cradle of his big arms.

The cat settled right in—and started to purr.

"*Aww,*" said Polly, suddenly teary-eyed. "*Aww,* look at that. She *knows,* Nick. She senses it. You're the human for her."

Nick stared down at the cat, which gazed trustingly up at him. "Hell," he said wearily, "you women are ganging up on me."

"You'll take her, then?"

He didn't answer for a long moment, a moment in which the only sound was Daisy's contented purr. Then, at last, he surrendered—marginally. "You'd better keep her here till the weekend, in case one of your neighbors shows up for her."

"And if no one does?"

Nick admitted defeat. "All right. If no one comes to get her, then I've got myself a damn cat."

No neighbors appeared the next day to claim the little cat.

That night, Daisy sat on Nick's lap as he and Polly argued over several poems by Erica Jong. Jenny surreptitiously observed him, thinking that the cat really did seem to like him. And come Friday night, whatever excuses he came up with, he would be taking Daisy home. The litter box would be gone from the corner of her kitchen and spaying and distemper shots would be his to worry about.

Maybe she felt just a little bit guilty, to be forcing an innocent animal on Nick, who, in all the years she'd known him, had never shown any more desire for a pet than he had for a wife.

But he had changed his mind lately about wanting a wife. Maybe he'd learn to love a pet as well.

And Jenny did feel that the cat would be good for Nick—something warm and alive that needed his care. He could read all the books ever written about love; he could study them, and argue with Polly about them. But at some point, he had to start practicing loving, start getting used to providing the day-to-day care and attention a live creature demanded.

"You take care of my cat, now," he teasingly told Jenny when he left that night.

Jenny's pulse started racing, as it too often did now when Nick spoke to her. She ignored the rapid beating of her foolish heart, promised she would take good care of Daisy—and told herself Nick's words were more proof that making him take the cat had been a good move.

Thursday night, after dinner, Jenny left Nick and Polly to their studies and drove over to her mother's condo to pick up the teaching aids that Kirsten had said she could borrow. Once they'd carried the two felt boards down to Jenny's car, Kirsten invited her in for a cup of decaf.

Jenny hesitated, feeling as if she ought to hurry home. But why rush? Nick would be there for at least another hour. He'd look after Polly. And if there was a problem they would call her on the cell phone she always carried in her purse. Back home, she'd only end up in the spare room, sitting at her desk, listening for the sound of his voice and calling herself a hundred kinds of fool.

Jenny followed her mother back up the stairs.

"Nick, I really think it's about time that you at least *tried* to contact her again."

Nick petted Daisy, who sat purring on his lap. The ball of fuzz arched her back. Her motor was going good. She really was a cute little thing. For a cat. And either Polly had given her a bath, or she'd started washing herself with that rough tongue of hers. Her striped orange coat had a nice clean look to it now.

"Nick. Did you hear what I said?"

He glanced up. "I told you. She said she didn't want to see me anymore."

"So?"

"So, I'm respecting her wishes. For a while."

Polly gave a little grunt of impatience. "Nick. You *have* to do something to get back with her. If you don't, I mean, what's the point of all this work that we're doing?"

Nick shifted in his chair a little. He didn't like the look in Polly's eyes at all. He wasn't ready to approach Sasha yet. It hadn't even been two weeks since she'd left him that note. A woman like Sasha needed her space. "I'll get a hold of her. When the time is right."

"And just when is that going to be?"

Nick petted the cat some more. He wished Jen hadn't taken off and left him alone here with just the kitten and a bossy thirteen-year-old.

"Nick. When?"

He glanced toward the kitchen, and up, at that skylight he'd put in a few years back. The only place he tried not to look was at Polly.

"Wait!" Polly said, with sudden and unnerving glee, "I have an idea."

Nick started shaking his head before she even finished the sentence. "I don't know, Pol..."

She gave him a look of pure disgust. "How can you shake your head like that? You haven't even heard it yet."

"Well, if it's got something to do with me calling Sasha—"

"You don't have to call her." Polly's cheeks were pink. Flushed. With excitement over this "idea" she'd just had.

Nick didn't like it. He didn't like it at all. He put on his most hangdog expression. "Look. She really crushed me, you know, when she dumped me? A guy has his pride. I don't want to try to talk to her. Not for a while. You can call me a coward and maybe I am, but—"

"Wait. That's just it. You don't have to *talk* to her. You don't have to say a word."

He held back a groan. "Flowers, right? You want me to send her a dozen red roses."

Polly was smiling so wide, all the metal in there gleamed. "No. Roses. Boring. And way too easy. Anyone can send roses."

He felt slightly offended. "Hey. Roses ain't cheap."

"Money. All you adults ever think about is how much something costs."

"It's easy to say that when you're thirteen and you have a mom like Jen, who keeps you warm and safe in a nice house and cooks you one hell of a hot meal every damn night.''

"Can we not talk about *dinner*. Please? This is about Sasha. About the woman you love." Somehow, when Polly called Sasha the woman he loved, it sounded laughable. He petted the cat some more and tried not to wonder why that might be. "Nick. You'd better be listening to me.''

"Okay, okay." Browbeaten, he was thinking. That's what I am. Browbeaten. By a thirteen-year-old.

Polly sat back in her chair and folded her arms over her chest. "A letter."

He lifted an eyebrow at her. "Huh?"

"A *love* letter." She jumped from her chair and pounded down the hall.

Nick sat there, petting the cat, kind of hoping she wouldn't come back.

No such luck. Here she came. *Clomp-clomp-clomp.* Skinny as a fence post, but still, the kid sounded like she weighed two hundred pounds when she ran. She skidded to a stop at his elbow and slid a few sheets of expensive-looking writing paper in front of him. Then she plunked a pen on top of the paper. "Give me Daisy and start writing."

He looked up at her. "You know, you're badgering me. That's what you're doing. I don't like it much."

"I want the cat."

He tried a little change of subject. "Nice paper." It was probably Jen's. She might not like Polly taking it without her permission. "Where'd you get it?"

"Grandma Brown sent it to me. For writing letters to her and Grandpa."

Andy's parents had retired to Tucson six or seven

years before. "Well. I'm glad to hear you keep in touch with them."

"Don't try to distract me. Give me that cat." She reached down and took Daisy away from him. Then, holding the cat in one hand, she picked up the pen with the other and jabbed it at him. He took it, just to keep from getting poked with it.

"Now," she said. "Just start writing. Write what you feel. Write what's in your heart."

Under his breath, he muttered a word he shouldn't have said.

"Don't swear. Write."

He looked down at those blank sheets of paper— and didn't have a clue where to start. "Polly, I really can't. Love letters just aren't my style."

She let out a sigh big enough to blow a strip mall sideways. "Oh, all right. I guess I'll have to help. I'll have to be your Cyrano."

"My what?"

"Your Cyrano. You know, Cyrano de Bergerac? That play by Rostand?"

Cyrano de Bergerac. It sounded vaguely familiar. Nick thought they'd made him read it in high school. "The guy with the big nose, right?"

Polly looked hopeful. "Then you've read it?"

"It was a while ago."

Another giant sigh. "Well, maybe we should have you read it again. Even if it is by a *man*. See, Cyrano loves his cousin, Roxanne. And he's an incredible man. He's this musician-poet-swordsman-philosopher."

"Quadruple threat, right? Everything a woman wants."

"You got it. But unfortunately—"

Nick nodded. "The giant schnoz. A real turnoff."

"He's afraid she could never love him. So he helps his friend, Christian, to woo her. By writing these fabulous letters, by telling Christian beautiful things to say to her. It works. But then Christian dies. And Cyrano swears never to reveal that he was the soul of the man Roxanne loved. Roxanne becomes a nun and—" She cut herself off in midsentence.

He tried to keep her going. "Go ahead. Tell me the rest."

She shook her head. "Never mind. Forget Cyrano for now. The point is, I'm going to help you with this letter you need to write."

Just the kind of help he *didn't* need. "Aw, Pol…"

"I mean it. This will work out just great." Her braces gleamed at him. "I'll write it for you. Then you can copy what I write, so it really will be from you."

He sincerely and truly did not like this idea. "I don't know, Pol…"

"Nick, it'll be what's in *your* heart. It'll only be my words—wait a minute." She whirled and ran off down the hall again, returning in thirty seconds with more blank paper.

He looked at her with extreme wariness. "What's that?"

"Scratch paper. For the rough draft. I'll write it on this paper. And then you can copy what I wrote onto the good stuff."

"It just doesn't sound…straight, you know? If I don't even write it, then—"

"Don't worry. You'll copy it, so it'll be in *your* handwriting. And I'll make it good. I promise, Nick.

It might take a while, but I'll get it just right. Trust me. Please. You're gonna be proud of it.'' She was shoving the cat at him again. ''Here. Take Daisy. And give me that pen.''

''Jennifer, is there something bothering you lately?''

Surprised at the question and suddenly very uncomfortable, Jenny stared across the table at the face that was a lot like her own: the same strong chin and blue eyes, the same light blond hair—hair so pale, it hardly showed the gray.

Her mother continued, ''You've seemed so... subdued the past couple of times we've talked. Subdued and a little preoccupied.'' Kirsten picked up her mug and drank, her eyes concerned and watchful over the rim of the cup. ''Are you troubled about this new man you're going out with tomorrow night?''

Jenny looked down into her own cup. A single word floated into her mind. Nick. She ordered it to float right back out. ''Mom, honestly. Roger's a nice man. But I'm not *troubled* about him, not at all.''

''It does seem that *something* is bothering you.''

Jenny wrapped her fingers around the cup handle, but then didn't pick it up. She confessed, softly, ''Maybe I am a little down.'' Then she forced a small laugh. ''That's pretty vague, huh?''

Kirsten nodded. ''Yes. But it's okay to be vague. And if you're feeling down, well, everyone has times like that. I just want you to know, if you need someone to talk to, I'm here.''

For some reason, Jenny found herself thinking of her father. Tom Lundquist had been a decade older than his wife. He'd died of a first heart attack nine years ago. The death, like Andrew's death, had taken them completely by surprise. Jenny's father had never smoked. He rarely drank and had stayed lean and fit.

"Mom?"

"Mmm?"

"You *seem* happy, living alone. But are you, really?"

Kirsten thought for a moment, then she replied, "The first year after your father died, that was the worst. I must confess, if I'd met someone then, some nice, friendly fellow with whom I could carry on an interesting conversation..." Kirsten shrugged and sipped more decaf.

"What? Tell me."

"Well, if I'd met such a man—and if that man had asked me—I would have said yes in a heartbeat."

Jenny sat back a little. "You're kidding." She didn't really intend to sound disapproving, but somehow it came out that way.

Her mother only smiled. "No. I'm quite serious. I was terribly lonely. I wanted a husband, to try to fill the huge gap your father had left. But no man appeared. No one asked. And as the years have gone by, I've come to enjoy my independence. I don't think I'd be willing to give it up now, even for a man as wonderful as your father was."

Jenny shook her head. "The first year after Andrew died, I couldn't even have *looked* at another man." Nick came drifting into her mind again. She ordered him away. "And I know how you felt about Dad. I think you're fooling yourself a little about this. If that man you described *had* come along, you wouldn't have married him. I just don't believe you could have done that."

"Jennifer," her mother chided, "I love you dearly. But we are two different people."

"Well, I know that." It came out sounding defensive, though she hadn't meant it to.

Her mother smiled. "Sometimes one needs reminding, even of the most obvious things."

Jenny glanced at her watch. Nick would be leaving soon. She really ought to get home. "So then. You're happy? As a single woman."

"Yes, I am. But I think the real question here is, are you?"

Jenny opened her mouth to say something brisk and final. But then her glance fell on the toaster, over on the counter by the stove. The blue toaster that matched the walls of her mother's kitchen exactly. Andrew had found that toaster. At Sears, shortly after Kirsten had moved in here. He'd brought it over and taken it out of the box and plugged it into the wall. If Jenny closed her eyes, she could still see him now.

Andrew in old sweats and a T-shirt, standing by the counter where the toaster sat gleaming. He'd been grinning with pride. "Well, Kirsten." He'd gestured with his long, lean arm, a sort of flourish, at the toaster. "What do you think?"

And her mother had answered, "I think that my daughter has married a very thoughtful man."

"Oh, Mom." Jenny didn't sound brisk at all. The words came out harsh and low. "I loved him so."

Across the table, her mother whispered, "I know."

"How could there be anyone else for me? It still hurts, just to think of him. I don't think I could take it, to love like that again—to open myself up like that again, all the time knowing just what it would be like, to *lose* like that again.''

Her mother said nothing. She simply reached out her hand. Jenny took it, gratitude washing through her, that her mother didn't say all the easy things, about taking a chance again, about getting past her fears. Jenny knew all those things. Hearing her mother say them wouldn't help her.

They sat there for what seemed to be a very long time, holding hands across the table.

Jenny was the one who pulled away at last. ''I should go. Nick's with Polly, but he'll be leaving soon.''

''I'm here. If you need me.''

''I know. And it helps.''

When Jenny arrived home, she found Nick and Polly in their usual seats at the table.

Polly had her head bent; she was writing something. Daisy sat in Nick's lap. Several sheets of blank paper were stacked in front of him. For a second, Jenny stared at the blank paper, frowning.

When she looked up, Nick was watching her. She felt that bothersome jolt of awareness that always took her by surprise now whenever he glanced her way. He smiled. ''Hey, Jen.''

Something wasn't right. He looked…uncomfortable. Maybe even a little bit embarrassed. That smile was…what? Sheepish. Yes. That was the word. She looked at him more sharply. He broke eye contact with her to gaze down at the kitten, which he then began petting.

Jenny could hear the low, contented purr. She watched Nick's big, tanned hand as it moved in slow, gentle strokes from the top of the orange head, down the fuzzy body, to the end of the striped tail, which the kitten had left uncurled so it draped over the hard curve of his thigh. Each stroke seemed to engulf the cat, since it was so small and Nick had such big hands.

All at once, in the middle of a stroke, he looked up and snared Jenny's glance again. Jenny felt a maddening, lazy warmth, down low in her belly.

She shook herself. "Hi, you two." Her voice sounded casual, and that pleased her. She felt one hundred percent certain that Nick had no clue of her new and disturbing reactions to him. "How's the training going?"

Nick got that look again: sheepish. "Uh, just fine."

Polly made some indecipherable noise and kept her head studiously bent over the paper she was scribbling on. She'd pulled the dining-room wastebasket close to her chair.

Puzzled, Jenny started for the hall. As she passed Polly's chair, she glanced down into the wastebasket. It was half full of wadded-up papers. Failed efforts, apparently.

But failed efforts at *what?*

She kept walking, to her bedroom, where she set her purse on the dresser and hung up her coat. Then she went and stood right by the open door to the hall. She listened.

Quiet. It was too quiet. The two of them should be arguing. And Nick should be laughing.

Then Nick spoke. "Let me read that."

"Just a minute."

''Pol, come on. You've been scribbling away for half an hour. Let me see.''

''I want to get it right. I want her to be *overwhelmed* with your depth and sensitivity. I need time to do that. You'll just have to wait.''

Just who, Jenny wondered, was supposed to be overwhelmed with Nick's depth and sensitivity?

She knew immediately: Sasha. The incredible, elusive, intellectual, cat-loving Sasha.

And how was that supposed to happen? By something Polly was writing, apparently. Something Polly just had to *get right*.

Jenny returned to the dining area and slid into the chair on Nick's left.

Nick sat up a little straighter, then granted her another in a growing series of uncomfortable smiles. Polly didn't even lift her head.

''What's going on here?''

Nick cleared his throat. ''Well, Jen, uh…'' His voice trailed off as the kitten jumped from his lap. It strutted toward the kitchen, orange tail high.

Jenny turned to her daughter. ''Polly, what are you writing?''

''Not now, Mom,'' Polly mumbled. ''I've got to get this right.''

Jenny shifted her glance to Nick again. She gazed at him levelly, waiting.

Finally he muttered, ''It's a letter.''

She waited some more, for him to further enlighten her. He didn't. So she prompted, ''A letter?''

''Yeah.''

''A letter to whom?''

At last he confessed what she'd already deduced. "To Sasha."

"What kind of a letter?"

He really looked miserable now. "Hell, Jen." He ran both hands over that thick, short-cropped hair of his, then let them fall to his sides with a heavy sigh.

"What kind of a letter, Nick?" Jenny's growing impatience with him made her tone sharp.

Polly deigned to glance up. She scowled. "Mother. I cannot think with you talking."

"I have asked Nick several times, and he seems hesitant to explain this to me. So I'll ask you. What kind of a letter are you writing?"

Polly gave a little snarl of pure impatience.

"Please do not snarl at me. Answer my question."

Polly glared, then snarled again, "That does it." She grabbed the paper she'd been writing on, wadded it into a ball and dropped it into the wastebasket beside her. "Thank you very much, Mother. I've totally lost it."

"Lost what?" Increasing exasperation sharpened Jenny's voice even more. She did not like her daughter's snotty behavior. She did not like the look on Nick's face. She did not like the way he kept avoiding her questions. "Something suspicious is going on here. And I want to know what."

Polly huffed, "I've lost my train of thought, Mother. You made me lose my entire train of thought."

"Do I have to dig around in that wastebasket to find out what you're talking about?"

"It's none of your business, Mother."

Jenny warned, too gently, "Watch your tone, young lady."

Polly huffed some more. "Mother. We are working here. You have interrupted us. You have no right to—"

"Settle down, Pol," Nick said bleakly. He ran a hand over his hair again, and let out a long breath. "Damn, this is embarrassing. It's a love letter. A love letter for me to send to Sasha."

A love letter. For him to send to Sasha.

The words seemed to echo in Jenny's brain as she stared at him, at his sexy dark eyes and his silver-kissed black hair, at his powerful, tanned neck and his too-broad shoulders. At all that *manliness*. Too much *manliness*.

All that manliness that was here, in her house, all the time now.

She didn't need all that manliness sitting at her table every night, tempting her to forget who she was, who *he* was, who they were to each other. Tempting her to indulge herself in certain…feelings. Certain danger-ous, impossible, terribly disturbing feelings that could never go anywhere, since he was in love with this woman named Sasha and she, Jenny, was—

No. Jenny pulled her raging thoughts up short. What was the matter with her? It was not Nick's fault that, out of nowhere, after all these years, she'd suddenly developed a thoroughly embarrassing *crush* on him.

She couldn't blame Nick for that. He'd done nothing at all to encourage her, beyond coming around five nights a week for these silly lessons in sensitivity and getting her thinking how handsome he was, getting her wondering about things she had no right to wonder about.

She simply had to keep her mind on the real issue here.

Which was that Polly had been writing passionate words for Nick to pass off as his own. To some woman Jenny didn't even know. Some woman totally unsuited to him who'd made it very clear that she was through with him.

Jenny glared at him. He stared back at her. His dark eyes seemed to get darker.

She wanted to scream. To jump on him and pound his chest and tell him to stop being such a complete fool. To stop being *him*, with his deep laugh and his big, comforting arms, his cat-stroking hands and his history of hot sex with women who were as unique as they were temporary in his life.

Overreacting.

She knew she was overreacting.

She said, very carefully, "I think you should write your own love letters, Nick."

Polly groaned. "Mother. He can't. He couldn't think of what to say. So I was helping him to—"

"—lie," Jenny finished for her, feeling way too self-righteous. "You were helping him to lie."

Polly let out an outraged cry. "This is unfair! It's not a lie. They were *his* feelings. I was just putting them in words."

"If Nick wants to write Sasha a love letter, he should write it himself."

"But I just *told* you. He *can't* write it. He can't think of what to say."

"Then fine. Leave it at that. It's one thing to get him reading love poetry and romantic novels. To have him studying self-help articles and poring over books on art. But it's something else again to put words into his mouth. That's not right. I forbid you to do that.''

Polly made a loud growling sound. "*Arrrgh.* You're just butting in on something you don't even understand. I am trying to *help* this man, and you're ruining everything.''

"A lie won't help him." Calm. She really did sound calm. Oh, she was glad for that. Because she did not feel calm.

"Mother, it is not a lie!"

"Polly." Nick's voice was low.

Polly swung on him. "What? *What?*"

"Your mother's right."

Chapter Eight

Out of proportion, Nick thought. This whole thing was getting blown way, way out of proportion. Polly was watching him, her face all red and her eyes wide and wounded, as if he'd double-crossed her. And Jen looked as if she wanted to knock out a few of his teeth.

He told Polly again, very gently, "Your mom is right. Writing a love letter is something I just have to do for myself."

Polly moaned. "But that's just it. You *won't* do it."

"Polly," Jen cut in, her voice drawn as tight as a chalked string. "That's enough. I've forbidden you to do this and Nick doesn't even *want* you to do this."

Polly whirled on her mother. "He does so. It's *you.* You butted in. You're the one who's—"

Jen didn't let her finish. "Polly. I said no."

Polly went rigid. Then she stood, shoving her chair

back so it tottered on two legs before it righted itself. "Fine. Ruin all our work. Ruin his life. Ruin *everything*. Go ahead."

Jen said nothing. Polly took a step and bumped into the wastebasket. With great dignity, the kid bent, picked up the basket and moved it aside. Then she walked away, down the hall, her head held very high. She walked quietly for once.

Nick waited. He knew damn well what would happen once she got past her bedroom door.

And it did.

She slammed it, hard.

The sound echoed through the house. Nick shot a glance at Jen. She looked ready to chew nails.

He eyed her for a moment, trying to figure out what he ought to say next.

He couldn't think of a single thing. Apparently, she couldn't either. So they just sat there. The air seemed to hum and vibrate between them, as it used to sometimes in the old days, back when they only put up with each other for Andy's sake.

Nick truly did hate having Jen mad at him. And he couldn't stand the damn silence. A remark popped into his mind and he said it. "That kid really knows how to slam a damn door."

Jen's lips were pursed so tight they looked white. "And whose fault is that, do you think?"

That bugged him, made him forget momentarily that he was trying to smooth things over. "Oh, right. Now it's my fault that your kid slams doors."

"You know what I mean, Nick. You know very well." She pushed each word out, low and hissy, through those tight lips.

He wanted to reach out and grab her, give her a good shake, until she loosened those lips and stopped glaring at him as if he was someone she wished she didn't know. But he didn't do that. Instead he tried for reason again. "Jen, you do let her walk all over you sometimes. You—"

"Nick DeSalvo. Don't you dare tell me how to raise my child."

"I'm not, damn it. I'm just saying that she needs—"

She threw up a hand, palm out, chopping the air with it. "Stop. I will not sit here and listen to *you* tell me what she needs. I will not." She slapped the table with that hand, shook her head and repeated, "I will not."

She looked so…confused. As if she didn't know any better than he did how they'd gotten here, fighting with each other over a letter that was never going to get written, anyway.

Something passed through him, something scary and tender, something that hurt. He spoke more gently, without even trying to. "Look. I'm sorry. This whole thing, this letter, it was a lousy idea."

"Exactly." She lowered her chin, stared down at her hand, flat there on the table. "Lying is a bad idea. Pretending you wrote something you didn't is a bad idea. And getting my daughter in on your little deception is a *really* bad idea."

He couldn't bear her anger. He wanted to make it go away. He reached across the distance between his chair and hers, needing to touch her, needing peace between them. "Jen…" His hand brushed her cheek.

"Don't." Her head shot up. "Don't…give me any excuses. I don't want to hear them." She pushed her chair back a little, getting farther away, as if his touch revolted her.

That urge took hold of him again, to grab her. To shake a little sense into her, until she softened and let him hold her, until she treated him once more like the real friend he knew that he was. He leaned closer to her, just a fraction, following that urge.

And she said it again, a command, "Don't. I mean it."

He retreated backward in his chair. It took everything he had in him, to do that.

There was a silence. A long one. He didn't understand it. Not any of it. How the thing with the letter had led to this: to Polly stalking off and shutting herself in her room. To Jen so mad at him that she wouldn't even let him touch her.

She had her head down again, as if she couldn't even look at him. "I think you'd better go home now. I think you've had about enough *training* for one week."

What did that mean? "Are you saying you don't want me to show up tomorrow?"

She raised her head, and pulled her shoulders straight. "Yes. I think you'd better stay away for a few days."

A few days. How long, exactly, was that? He had to know. He asked, with heavy sarcasm, "Do I have your *permission* to come back on Monday?"

She waved a hand, a tired kind of gesture. "Oh, Nick. Come on. Do you honestly believe that this training thing is doing any good?"

He answered without hesitation, "Yeah. I do. I think

it's helping me a lot.'' And it was—though maybe not in the way he'd expected at first.

Damn it, he really *liked* what had been going on around here the past couple of weeks. Liked watching Jen in the kitchen. Liked the hot, home-cooked meals that they shared as if they were a family. Liked arguing with Polly. Liked all of it. Very much.

He'd stay away till Monday, if Jen said he had to. He'd give them all a chance to cool off, to get past this mess that had happened tonight. But Monday was it. He'd be back then. In time for dinner. He'd make sure that Jen had forgiven him and he'd have a talk with Polly about controlling her temper.

''All right,'' Jen said, sounding worn-out. ''You can come back on Monday.'' She waved her hand again, dismissing him. ''But now, I mean it. You go on. Go home.''

The way she said that made him feel like some stray dog. Some mangy mutt she'd found lifting its leg on her lawn, something she didn't have time for. Some creature she was shooing away.

Okay, so he'd messed up. He never should have let Polly get going on that letter in the first place. But did a minor mistake like that give Jen the right to treat him like a stray mutt? To put that snooty tone in her voice? That tone he remembered damn well, now he thought about it.

She used to get that tone with him all the time—in the old days. Whenever he and Andy wanted to shoot a few hoops together, or step out for a beer. Or do anything that didn't include Her Majesty, the snow queen.

The snow queen. God, he'd forgotten that.

He'd secretly called her that for years. Snow queen. With her blond hair and her fine white skin, and those blue eyes that gave him icy, superior looks. Yeah, she used to freeze him out like this all the time.

Nick shoved back his chair, watched her wince at the abrupt sound, felt a small flare of satisfaction. Yeah, fine. He'd screwed up and she just had to make him pay for it. Make him squirm and fall all over himself trying to tell her how damn sorry he was. And now she jumped like a scared rabbit when he made a sudden move, so *sensitive* to his vulgar, masculine ways.

"You know." He loomed over her. "You're making a hell of a big deal out of something pretty damn small."

Her head shot up. Two bright spots of color stained those high, delicate cheekbones. He saw it in her eyes: shame. The awareness that she really had pushed this thing too far.

His frustration with her faded again. All he wanted was to touch her, to find some way to make everything instantly right.

But things *weren't* right. And if she wouldn't let him get near her, he couldn't make them right.

"I'll be back on Monday." He gave her the words as both a threat and a promise.

She sighed. "Yes. Monday. All right."

"We'll…work this out then."

"Whatever. That's fine."

He turned and started for the door.

She spoke to his back. "Nick."

Hope—like some bright, warm light in a window

late at night—switched on inside him. He turned back. "Yeah?"

"Better take Daisy with you."

The bright light went dark.

"Nick, you did say you'd take her, on the weekend."

"I know what I said."

"Well, then. Since you won't be back tomorrow, you'd better go ahead and take her now."

As if she knew who they were talking about, the little cat appeared, peeking around the kitchen doorway at them. Nick met those curious, golden eyes, then glanced at Jen again.

She stared right back at him. Patient. Unwavering.

The cat tiptoed over to him, sat down. *"Rreow?"*

"Fine," he growled, "I'll take the damn cat."

Chapter Nine

The minute the door clicked shut behind Nick and little Daisy, Jenny wanted to call them back.

She heard Nick's words in her mind: You're making a hell of a big deal out of something pretty damn small.

He was right.

She'd jumped at the chance to blame him. And she'd used her trumped-up anger as an excuse to send him away, to give herself a little breather from his nearness, a little distance from him, a few days where she didn't have to deal with her dear friend who had suddenly managed to become the object of her crazy, disorienting, inappropriate infatuation.

Well, she'd gotten her breather.

But she hadn't been fair.

And she knew it.

She should tell him as much. She should wait until

he had time to get home and then call him and tell him—

What?

That she longed to join the ranks of the flugel player, the lady biker and the feminist performance artist? That she couldn't watch him pet a cat without that loosening, heating sensation in the pit of her stomach? That she was *jealous* of Sasha? That if he was going to try to write a love letter, she wanted it addressed to her?

Oh, no.

She couldn't tell him things like that.

And she wouldn't tell him things like that.

This crush of hers would fade. She knew it. She would go out with Roger tomorrow night, and have a good time. She would get some *perspective* on these irrational feelings she had for Nick.

And when Nick returned on Monday night, she'd apologize for overreacting. She'd say she'd had a…headache. Yes. That she hadn't been feeling well and she'd taken it out on him. She'd ask him to forgive her.

And they'd put tonight behind them, once and for all.

"Nick left, huh?"

Jenny turned to see her daughter, standing right behind her. Polly had her hands in the pockets of her faded wide-leg jeans. "I heard the front door close."

"Yes. Well, you're right. Nick is gone."

Polly looked down at her shoes. "Mom?"

Jenny waited. She knew the beginnings of an apology when she heard one.

"I guess I was kind of a creep, about this letter thing."

Jenny kept her expression grave. "Yes. You were definitely a creep."

Polly slid into the chair next to Jenny, the one Nick had been sitting in a few minutes before. "Mom. I want to help him. I...I think I'm really good at this, you know?"

"Good at what?"

"Helping people. To work out their romantic problems."

Jenny wondered about her choice of words. "Helping *people?* Is there someone else you're giving romantic advice to?"

Polly's eyes went vague. "Someone else?"

"Yes, Polly. Someone else."

"Oh, Mom. All I meant is, I think I'm good at it. I think I'm really helping Nick. And I guess I got too...enthusiastic, about that love letter. I didn't stop to think that it wasn't honest, to write it for him." She hunched her shoulders, and pressed both hands between her knees. "I guess I'm sorry." She looked at Jenny, adorably contrite. Jenny melted inside, though she knew she probably shouldn't. "I mean it, Mom. I was a creep and I'm sorry and I'll try not to be like that again."

Jenny reached out and brushed a swatch of brown hair out of Polly's eyes. "All right. We'll let it go."

"Thanks, Mom."

"You're welcome."

Polly turned in her chair. "Where's Daisy?" She began calling. "Daisy. Here, Daisy..."

"She's gone, honey."

Polly swung back to her mother. "Huh?"

"Nick took her home with him."

"But why? He wasn't going to take her until tomorrow."

"He's not coming tomorrow."

Polly's face fell. "Why?"

"I was angry. I told him he'd had enough training for one week."

"But—"

"Honey, he'll be back on Monday. And anyway, your grandmother's coming tomorrow night."

"So?"

"So, I won't be here. You two can play that MindTrap game, or Scrabble. Spend a little time together."

"Wait a minute. Where are *you* going?"

Somewhat reluctantly, Jenny admitted, "I have a date."

Polly forgot all about Nick as she absorbed that bit of information. "*You? A date?*"

"Yes."

"With who?"

"A nice man who works at my school. His name's Roger. He teaches fifth grade."

"Wow. A date. My mom on a date. Weird." Polly leaned forward. "Hey. If you need a few pointers, you know, on the whole dating thing, I'm always here. And don't look at me like that. I told you. I've got a talent for—"

The phone rang.

Polly leapt from the chair. "I'll get it. I'm sure it's Mellie." She pounded off down the hall.

* * *

"Your mother seems nice," Roger said. They were sitting in the dim theater, waiting for the movie to start. "And your daughter, too."

"Thank you. I think they're both pretty terrific."

"I hated my wife's mother," Roger said. "Classic evil mother-in-law syndrome. She was a lot of our problem—mine and my ex-wife's."

Jenny sipped from the Coke she'd picked up at the snack bar on their way in. So far, the date was going well. Jenny didn't feel nervous at all. "Come on, Roger. You don't really mean that your ex-mother-in-law was *evil,* do you?"

He laughed and tossed a few chocolate covered raisins into his mouth. "She was. She is. Definitely. The devil incarnate."

"I don't believe that."

He shrugged. "I'm not going to go into detail. It would ruin the evening. Did *you* like *your* mother-in-law?"

"Yes, we always got along quite well, as a matter of fact."

"What about your father-in-law?"

"Adored him."

"Next you're going to say that your husband and your mother never shared a harsh word."

"I wouldn't go that far. People in families do have their differences. But they really did like each other a lot."

"I can't stand this. Perfect in-laws. It's not normal and you know it." Roger laughed again, and she laughed, too. The lights dimmed. Popcorn boxes and beverage containers began to dance across the screen.

Jenny settled back in her seat, a little relieved that

the show had started. She'd been just about to mention Nick, her husband's best friend, whom she'd barely tolerated for over a decade—and who had ended up becoming her own dearest friend.

Her dearest friend—and now something scarily more.

Not that she would have mentioned that part to Roger.

But still, it was better not to go into the subject of Nick at all.

With a muttered curse, Nick tossed the magazine across the room. It landed in front of the black slate fireplace where a gas fire pretended to burn a pair of big fake logs.

Daisy, batting at a catnip-stuffed mouse a few feet from where the magazine landed, jumped straight up in the air and then darted off across the beige marble floor, slipping and sliding all the way, to hide behind a chair.

Nick cursed again, more softly. He glanced at the stack of magazines on the side table at his elbow. Women's magazines. Much like the one he'd just thrown at the fireplace.

Magazines chock-full of helpful hints on how to get love and make it work and never let it fade.

Why was he reading these things anyway?

And on Friday-damn-night, no less.

Because Polly Brown, his own personal expert on love, had told him to.

He rested an elbow on the stack of magazines and then leaned on it. The one-handed clock built into the slab of slate that extended to the vaulted ceiling above the fireplace said it was eight-fifteen. Or thereabouts. Who could ever be one hundred percent sure of the time, with a one-handed clock? He'd thought the clock was interesting, when he'd first seen it. Now he just thought it was stupid; a clock with one hand missing.

With golden eyes round as two pennies, Daisy peeked out at him from behind the chrome-and-black-leather chair where she'd scooted when the magazine hit.

"Sorry 'bout that," he said. "Didn't mean to scare you."

"Rreow?"

He put up both hands. "Look. I'm a little edgy here, you know what I mean?"

The kitten stepped out from behind the chair, plunked herself down and started giving herself a bath.

Nick let out a gusty sigh, picked up another magazine—and then dropped it back on the stack.

Maybe he should try one of those videos Polly had recommended. *Pretty Woman* or *Pride and Prejudice.*

He let out a low groan. He'd rather stare at a one-handed clock than watch some love story right now.

The TV remote sat on the couch beside him. He grabbed it up and pointed it at the giant screen across the room. There had to be a basketball game on one of the sixty-odd channels his satellite dish pulled in.

After five minutes of surfing, he found one. Pistons versus the Denver Nuggets. He watched for a while. But it was a rout. He switched the set off, tossed the remote down and glanced at the clock again. Eight forty-five, approximately.

He wondered what Jen and Polly were doing. If Jen hadn't kicked him out and told him not to come back till Monday, he'd know what they were doing. Because he'd be over at their house. Where the floors had carpets on them, for pity's sake. Where the clocks were normal clocks, either digital or with two hands. Where things *smelled* like people lived there.

Maybe he just ought to get good and drunk.

Rising, he crossed the acres of gleaming bare floor, went down a hall and into the kitchen. He flicked on the lights. The steel stove and refrigerator, the yards and yards of Corian counters, gleamed at him. A guy could do surgery in here, it was so clean and bare.

Yeah, he really did need to think about selling this place. About finding himself something more homey, some place where the kitchen didn't remind him of an operating room. If it wasn't eight forty-something on Friday night, he'd call up a Realtor right now.

He stalked over to the fridge, pulled it open and stared at the cans of Millers lined up on the bottom shelf. He bent to reach for one—and then straightened without picking it up.

"Friday-damn-night," he growled. "All by my lonesome on Friday-damn-night and nothing but the Pistons versus the Nuggets on my sixty-odd channel giant-screen TV." All because of Jen. Because Jen had decided to remind him why he used to hate her so much.

Nick shoved the refrigerator door shut.

Nobody had to be alone on Friday night. Not as long as there were places like the Nine-Seventeen Club around.

After the movie, Roger asked if Jenny would like to stop somewhere for coffee.

They found a nice little coffee bar with round tables and bentwood chairs and ferns hanging everywhere. Jenny had a cappuccino. Roger chose something called 49er Blend. They sat at one of the round tables and sipped and talked—about the movie, about how Roger was adjusting to being single again, about the kids in their classes and the new principal, who'd taken over just that year and who showed a disturbing reluctance to back the teachers when problem students required disciplinary action.

"I'm glad we did this, Jenny," Roger told her.

She smiled across the table at him and made a noise of agreement.

She was thinking that she liked him. And that the evening had turned out just fine, easy and comfortable. Fun—in a safe, rather bland sort of way.

"We'll have to do it again."

She nodded, thinking, why not? Why shouldn't they do it again?

And that made her think of Nick. Of the way her heart raced whenever she saw him now.

It somehow made her feel *guilty*.

As if this date was a betrayal of what she felt for Nick.

Which was ridiculous, since what she felt for Nick was something she did not want to feel and intended to get over, very soon now.

"More cappuccino?" Roger asked.

Jenny said she would love one more cup.

The Nine-Seventeen Club was named after its address: 917 Exposition Boulevard. It had a pretty good-size parking lot—which was packed on Friday night.

Nick had to drive around for fifteen minutes, just to get himself a space.

Inside, the huge bar took up all of one long wall. The floor was dotted with small tables, every one of them taken. High counters and stools, all of them occupied, lined the other three walls. Tucked into a corner, not far from one end of the bar, a DJ sat on a dais and played country and soft rock just a little too loud.

Nick worked his way through the crush of people to the bar. He ordered a Scotch and soda. The bartender had just set the drink in front of him when the woman on the stool right next to him leaned over and shouted in his ear.

"Hi."

He turned her way, raised his drink to her and then sipped. She had soft brown hair and full lips and a very friendly look in her eye.

"I'm Louise," she said. "You come here often?"

He wondered, Why did they always ask that? Like it mattered.

But he knew his line. "Every once in a while."

"It's a little loud."

"Sure is."

She leaned her head on her hand and looked at him dreamily.

He knew what was coming next. Knew the whole conversation, just as it would go: What do you *do?* Oh, really? How *interesting…*

He smiled at Louise, who seemed nice and looked good and in whom he had absolutely no interest at all.

What in hell had possessed him to come here?

Beyond Louise's pretty brown head, way down at the other end of the bar, he saw Sasha.

He blinked, looked again.

Yeah. Wild red hair and that quick, nervous way of tipping her head to the side.

She hadn't seen him. A big guy leaned close to her. A rough trade sort of guy, with long black hair clubbed into a ponytail between his huge shoulders and arms like concrete pilings.

Nick stared as Sasha threw back her wild red head and laughed. The big guy leaned closer to her. She put her hand on his arm, and gave it a squeeze.

The truth dawned for Nick, standing there in the Nine-Seventeen Club, with his Scotch and soda in his hand and a pretty brunette named Louise watching him breathlessly, waiting for her opening to ask, What's your sign?

Sasha never really loved him, no matter what she had told him. Sasha was not looking for a husband at all. Nick was not the first lunkhead she'd met in a bar.

And he sure as hell wouldn't be the last.

He was probably damn lucky he'd always had sense enough to practice safe sex with her.

Louise shouted, "What's your name?"

"Nick."

The big guy put that huge arm around Sasha. She turned fully toward him, away from Nick, without ever once glancing over and catching sight of him there.

"Well, Nick. Can I buy you another drink?"

He set his glass down on the bar, gave Louise a final smile. "Thanks, but I just realized I gotta go."

"But—"

"Have a great time, Louise. Seriously." He turned and elbowed his way to the door.

Outside, the night air felt good. Fresh, cold and

clean. He gulped in a lungful of it and stared up at the three-quarter moon and he thought, Sasha Overfield is *not* the woman for me.

What a relief.

To finally let himself admit the damn truth.

Yeah, that was what he felt. Relief. That he could stop telling himself this lie about a woman he didn't even really know.

Why he'd thought he had to tell himself such a lie in the first place was another question—one he didn't really have an answer to. But that was okay. A guy didn't have to have the answer to every damn question that popped into his head.

He wanted to get into his car and drive straight to Jen's house. He wanted to tell her all about this…revelation he'd just had. Tell her how Sasha didn't love him, after all—and he didn't love her. How he felt so good and light and free, to admit the truth at last.

But Jen was mad at him.

That good feeling of lightness blew away on the night wind.

Left him lonely and down and thinking of his big, ugly house with its beige marble floors and black slate fireplace. Of that stupid clock with one hand.

The only thing alive in there was the fuzz ball. Who was probably wandering around from room to room, looking for her catnip mouse and meowing in self-pity, wondering why she'd had to get stuck with a lousy owner like him.

He should go home to her.

And he would. Soon.

But first, maybe he'd drive by Jen's house, see if he could drum up the nerve to knock on the door....

Nick pulled his car to a stop a few houses down from Jen's place, in the shadow of a big live oak. He turned off the engine and sat there for a moment, wondering what he was doing. Sitting in the shadows down the street from Jen's house at ten-thirty at night.

Words like sneaking and lurking came immediately to mind. Words like skulking and spying.

But he wasn't spying, not really. He just hadn't made up his mind yet if he was actually going to go up and knock on her door. And until he did make up his mind, he didn't want Jen to glance out a window and see him there.

As Nick sat in the shadows, trying to drum up the nerve to go up Jen's front walk and knock on her door, a light-colored late-model sedan came around the corner and parked in her driveway. A man got out, went around to the passenger side and pulled open the door. The woman inside the car swung her legs to the driveway and stood.

It was Jen.

Jen. With some guy Nick didn't think he'd ever seen before.

The guy closed the door and he and Jen walked around the front of the car. A moment later, they moved out of Nick's line of sight as they went up the front walk.

Nick sat very still. It took every ounce of willpower he possessed not to get out of the car and creep through the shadows to the top of Jen's driveway, where he could see if Jen and the strange man were still standing on the porch, or if they had gone inside.

The man appeared again, around the corner of the garage. He got into the car, started it up and backed into the street and drove away.

Nick just sat there, in his black Cadillac in the dark, wondering what the hell was going on.

A date? It sure looked like a date.

Jen on a date?

No. Jen didn't date. Jen had never gotten over Andy. Hadn't Nick seen her himself, just two weeks ago, with misty eyes and a glass of Chenin Blanc, poring over those old pictures of Andy, trying to get past one more anniversary of his death?

And besides, Jen and Nick were *friends*.

She would have told him if she'd started going out again.

Wouldn't she?

He felt kind of hurt, now that he thought about it. First, she'd played the damn snow queen again, kicked him out and told him not to come back until Monday. And now, here she was giving him reason to suspect she'd been out on a date with some guy he didn't even know.

He needed to talk to her about it. He needed to talk to her about lots of things. About Sasha, and how he'd figured out he didn't love her, after all. About last night and how damn unreasonable she'd been. And about this guy who'd just brought her home.

Who the hell was this guy?

Nick leaned on the car door, started to get out.

But then he changed his mind. He shut the door, still inside.

She'd told him Monday. He could come back on Monday.

Fine. Okay. He'd talk to her Monday.

Nick turned the key. The car hummed to life.

He had one more friend to visit tonight. The best kind of friend: one who would never send him away.

Chapter Ten

"Well? How did it go? Was it *fun?* He seemed okay. Do you *like* him? You're kind of early, aren't you?" Polly stood in the hallway, dressed in her plaid pajamas and smelling of toothpaste and Ivory soap.

Jenny pointed at the closed door to the spare room and whispered, "Granny in bed?"

"Yep. Crashed out. You know how she is. Talk to me, Mom. I want to hear it all."

Jenny went into her own room, where she flicked on the floor lamp and tossed her purse on the bed. She shrugged out of her jacket, thinking of last Saturday, of how that night she'd expected the third degree from Polly, and instead had found her zoned out in front of the tube. Now, tonight, for some reason, Polly just had to know everything. Kids were way too much like the rest of life: hard to predict.

Polly had followed her into the room, shut the door, shoved Jenny's purse aside and flopped down on the bed. "Mo-ther. Talk. Tell me. How *was* it?"

"There really isn't that much to tell. We both liked the movie. We stopped for coffee afterward."

Polly stretched out on her side, braced her head on her hand and let out a loud fake snore. "Wake me up when you get to the good part."

Jenny went to the closet and hung up her coat. "It was…very nice."

"Ugh," Polly said. "Nice. You worry me, Mom."

"Roger is a friend. A good friend. It's nothing…romantic."

"Just like Nick, right?"

No, Jenny thought guiltily. Not like Nick. Not like Nick at all…

"Mom. It's good that you're dating."

"Well, I'm so relieved to have your approval."

"But you're going to have to get past this *friend* thing, you really are."

"Who says I have to get past it?"

Polly rolled to her back and groaned long and loud. "Oh, Mom. You are hopeless. You honestly are."

Jenny sat on the bed and leaned over her daughter. "So. You've heard all about *my* date. Tell me how the plans are going for yours."

Polly rolled her eyes. "Mo-ther. It is not a *date*. It's a party. Mellie and I are going to a party."

"A boy-girl party, right?"

"Oh, please. *Boy-girl?* You make it sound totally grotesque."

"Oh, my. So sorry. What will you wear?"

"It's casual, Mom. Jeans. A T-shirt. Really. It's just

no big deal.'' She rolled to her stomach, put her head on her arms and spoke to the bedspread. ''Mellie's dad said he'd come and pick me up about lunchtime tomorrow.''

Jenny grinned. ''So that you and Amelia can take all afternoon getting ready?''

Another groan. ''Honestly. I just want to go to her house a little early. All right?''

''Sure. And I'll pick you up about eleven Sunday. How's that?''

''Mom. We might want to sleep in late, you know?''

''Eleven o'clock is quite late enough.''

Polly rolled to her back again and wrinkled her nose at Jenny. ''Oh, all right. Eleven. If you just *have* to.''

''I do. I just *have* to. And now, if you don't mind, I'd like to get a little sleep myself.''

Polly sat up. ''You mean like, get lost?''

''I mean like, good night.''

With more groaning, Polly dragged herself to her feet and trudged out the door.

The cemetery where Andy was buried had no fence around it. It did have sloping, thick lawns, a narrow creek with a little redwood bridge arching over it and plenty of trees—oaks and maples; weeping willows, too. Most of the trees were beginning to leaf out now. But the grounds still seemed pretty bare, especially at night, with everything dark and deserted-looking.

Nick parked his car in the lot by the funeral chapel and then walked along a pebbled path, across the redwood bridge to Andy's grave.

When he got there, he did what he always did.

First, he read the gravestone—a nice gray-spotted

black marble one that he and Jen had bought together. With the moon shining down, Nick could make out the words on it. But it didn't really matter if he could actually see them.

He knew them by heart. They read, Andrew Jonas Brown, with the dates below the name. At the bottom, in Roman-looking script, it said: Husband Father Son Friend

Nick really loved that. Husband, father, son—and friend. Andy had been all those things. And he'd been damn good at all of them, too.

Nick backed up, until he could sit on the little stone bench a couple of yards away from the foot of the grave. He shot a quick glance around—just to be sure no one else had decided to wander the pebbled paths on Friday night.

Reassured he was alone, he asked the gravestone, ''Well, bud, how you been?''

He stopped, listened. He often felt that Andy talked to him when he came here. It was corny and maybe a little bit spooky. But what the hell? His conversations with Andy were his own business. Nobody else had to know.

He came here once a month or so on average. The last time had been only two weeks ago. The night that Sasha had dumped him, the fourth anniversary of Andy's death. He'd come here and he'd talked to Andy. He really had felt as if he'd heard Andy's voice that night.

Go on over to our house, the voice had seemed to say. *Talk to Jenny. She'll help you.*

He'd hedged, ''Hey, bud. It's pretty damn late. I shouldn't be bothering your wife at this hour.''

The time doesn't matter, Andy said in a whisper that was probably only the wind. *Doesn't matter at all. Go to Jenny.*

So he'd gone.

The idea that Jenny might help him be a better man had come later, while he was telling her about Sasha and the kind of woman Sasha was.

Or at least, the kind of woman he had made himself believe that Sasha was.

The night breeze blew a dead leaf across the grass in front of Nick. He watched the leaf tumble on by. Then he heard rustling. He looked up and saw a bird take flight from a spindly-looking tree a few feet away. The bird swooped down and perched on Andy's gravestone. It folded its wings, tipped its head to the side and looked right at Nick.

A robin. Nick could clearly see the orange breast. Strange. He didn't think robins came out at night as a rule.

But there it was. Definitely a robin, peering at Nick through its little beady eye. Finally, without making a sound, it took off. Nick watched until it disappeared from sight. Then he looked at the gravestone again.

Hey Nick, Andy would say if he were here right now. *I'm doing okay. How 'bout you?*

Nick let out a long breath. "Not so good. Not really."

What's got you down?

"Well I'm kind of at loose ends, you know? I figured out tonight that I don't love Sasha." Another leaf blew by. Nick reached out, snatched it from the air as the wind lifted it off the walk. "But I guess you already knew that, didn't you?" He let the leaf go. It dropped to the grass, quivered there for a moment, then went still as the breeze died down. "Hell. I probably knew it myself. Just didn't want to see it. I realized I'm ready. For more than a few laughs and good sex. I decided Sasha should be ready, too." He laughed, at the night and the silent gravestone, at his own idiocy. "Right. I know. You don't have to say it. I never was the brightest guy around."

Nick bent and captured the leaf once more. He crumpled it in his fist and then brushed the dry leaf crumbs from his palm. "I think your wife's stepping out on you."

The breeze rose up again. *Pretty hard to step out on a dead man, Nick.*

Nick flinched. "You know, it gets me down when you call yourself a dead man."

It's only the truth.

"Damn it. I know." Nick sat forward, and braced his forearms on his knees. He looked at Andy's gravestone long and hard. And then he really started talking.

He told Andy all of it—everything that had happened since the last time he'd come here. About how he'd begged Jen to help him out and she had refused. But Polly had stepped in.

"So I've been getting training. *Sensitivity* training. Believe it. It's true. I'm getting in touch with my feminine side. Or so your daughter tells me. And I've got a cat. Can you feature that? Me with a damn cat. Polly named her Daisy. You know I would have chosen something else, if I'd *had* a choice. But those women. They ganged up on me. You know how they are."

He went on, told all of it. About the love letter that Polly had tried to write for him. About how Jen had kicked him out. About spotting Sasha in the Nine-Seventeen Club. About driving to Jen's and seeing her with that strange guy.

When he'd told it all, he waited a while.

But it didn't seem to him that Andy said anything.

The wind got a little stronger, got a bite to it. Nick turned up the collar of his leather jacket and hunched down a little, trying to get warm.

But it was no good. It kept getting colder and his dead friend had nothing to say.

Nick got up, stuck his hands into his pockets and walked back across the redwood bridge to his car.

At his house, the fuzz ball was waiting just inside the door. She meowed in greeting and rubbed herself around his ankles. He scooped her up and listened to her motor going.

"Glad to see me, are ya? It's good to know that *somebody* is."

He carried her on into the master suite, where he set her down on the floor and headed for a hot shower. When he came back into the bedroom, he found her curled up on the king-size bed. She lifted her head, stared at him and yawned. Nick climbed in under the big comforter. He heard the sound of purring in his dreams.

When Nick woke up the next morning, he knew he wouldn't last till Monday. He wanted things worked out with Jen. She really was an important friend to him. Probably his *best* friend, in the last few years since Andy was gone.

Friends—best friends especially—shouldn't be mad at each other.

He went to his office for a couple of hours in the morning, to catch up on a few things he'd been putting off. By noon, he was back at his house. He fed the fuzz ball and then he picked up the phone and dialed Jen's number.

She answered on the second ring. "Hello?"

He gulped, then very quietly put the phone back down.

A total jerk-wad thing to do. To call someone and hang up when they answered. He didn't know what was wrong with him. He never did things like that.

But then, he never did things like parking under the shadow of an oak tree down the street from someone's house at ten-thirty at night, either. Parking and just sitting there, in the dark, watching that someone come home from a date—or something that looked a damn lot like a date.

He picked up the phone again. And put it down.

No. Calling wouldn't do it. He had to see her face-to-face.

"Rreow?"

Daisy was sitting a few feet away, looking at him expectantly.

"What? You wanna go, too?"

"Rreow."

It occurred to him that showing up with the cat in his arms might just make him look more appealing. More sensitive. More the type of guy that Jen would let in her house on a Saturday, even though she'd told him not to show up till Monday.

"All right, you can come."

The cat seemed to smile.

Who said he wasn't sensitive? He talked to cats. He

talked to *dead* people. How the hell could a guy get more sensitive than that?

The smoke alarm lay on the kitchen table. Jenny stood over it, holding a 9-volt battery in one hand and the connecting wires in the other, wondering why the darn connectors wouldn't fit over the little knobs at the end of the battery, wishing Nick were there to snap the thing together, stick the battery right into its slot and put the whole thing back on the wall with a minimum of effort and thought.

It wasn't that she *couldn't* put a new battery in a smoke alarm. It was only that it *should* have been so simple. She felt like an idiot, because she couldn't even seem to match up the terminals correctly.

She brought the battery closer, peered at the tiny plus and minus at the bases of the little knobs that were supposed to hook up to the whatchamacallits on the end of the alarm wires. Yes. She had it right. She did.

But still, the thing wouldn't snap together.

She set the battery on the table and glared at it.

And thought of Nick again.

Wondered what he was doing now. Wondered if he was mad at her, because she'd made such an issue over that letter, if he was thinking bad thoughts about her since she'd told him to stay out of her sight for three days. Wondered, on the other hand, if he'd put her from his mind the minute he walked out her door. If he hadn't given her a thought in the past thirty-nine hours and forty-two minutes.

She didn't know which alternative bothered her more.

Actually, this morning she'd really wanted to call

him. She'd woken up and looked out the window and seen that it would be a sunny day, that there was a robin on the lawn, which always seemed to her a sign that the day would be good. Right then, she'd thought, This is ridiculous, this whole thing. I've treated Nick badly and I should have apologized right away. I shouldn't be putting it off till Monday. That's a cowardly thing to do.

She had gone so far as to pick up the phone. But then she'd put it down without dialing.

Coward. That's what she was.

In fact, when the phone had rung about twenty minutes ago, her heart had started hammering away, *boom-boom-boom,* in her chest. She'd been absolutely certain it was going to be Nick.

But whoever it was had hung up without speaking.

Her heart had settled down and she'd felt silly and just slightly depressed.

Jenny picked up the battery again, and scowled at the little knobs on the end of it. Yes, she did feel a little depressed. A little like a failure at life, somehow. A woman who picked fights with her dearest friend. A woman who couldn't even get the doohickeys on a smoke alarm to hook up to the battery watchamacallits.

The doorbell rang.

There went her heart again, *boom-boom-boom-boom.*

She set down the battery, ran a nervous hand back over her hair and checked to make sure her camp shirt was tucked neatly into her jeans.

When she pulled open the door, there he was, holding Daisy in his big arms, looking sheepish and sweet—as if he thought *he* was the one who should apologize for Thursday night.

"I'm sorry," he said. "I was a jerk."

Over the throbbing of her heart, she insisted, "No. I overreacted. Oh, Nick. I'm sorry, too."

They stared at each other.

All she could think was how good it was to see him.

And all Nick could think was that if he didn't have the fuzz ball purring away in his arms, he could reach for her. He could pull her close and—

By God. He wanted to *kiss* her.

And not just a good-friends peck on the cheek.

Oh, no. He wanted to put his mouth right on her mouth. To run his tongue along the little seam where her lips met, until she gave in and opened for him.

He wanted to feel her sigh into his mouth.

He wanted...

Jen.

That was it.

He wanted Jen.

Chapter Eleven

Like a bright light bursting on in a darkened room, the realization hit him.

He wanted Jen. He'd wanted Jen for a while now. And not let himself see it. He'd wanted her since...before he'd met Sasha.

And that had been the whole *point* of Sasha, hadn't it, really?

To distract him from having to admit to himself that he wanted Jen.

Because Jen was Andy's girl. And no guy worth anything made a move on his best friend's wife.

I'm dead, Nick. Deal with it, that's what Andy would say.

And Nick realized he *could* deal with it. He wanted to deal with it, was ready to deal with it.

But Jen. Could *she?*

Jen reached out and petted Daisy. In the process, the side of her hand brushed his chest. He felt the light touch all through him. The little cat purred even louder.

"I suppose you want to come in," she said, kind of playfully.

He could do playful. He teased back, "That was pretty much my goal, here. You wouldn't want to be the kind of woman who'd keep a man from reaching his goal, would you?"

"No, of course not. I would never want that." She was smiling, her mouth all soft and her eyes kind of wide and tender-looking. Her breathing seemed a little shallow, a little fast.

Like she was more than just glad to see him.

Like finding him on her doorstep had made her day.

"Well, come on in, then," she said at last. She stepped out of the way and he went through the door, then followed behind her into the kitchen. He leaned against the counter there, petting the purring kitten, as she disappeared into the garage, returning a moment later with the litter box and the two cat bowls—one for water and one for food.

"You went off without these the other night," she said, as she put the cat box in the corner.

"Yeah, I didn't remember them till I was halfway to my house. Had to find a pet store. It wasn't easy, that time of night."

She picked up one of the bowls and filled it with water, sending him another guilty glance in the process. "Sorry." She set the water bowl on the floor and rose to her feet again.

"You're forgiven." He put Daisy down.

The cat trotted right over and began lapping up a drink of water. Jen stood above her, with her arms wrapped around herself, watching the kitten. Since she wasn't looking his way, Nick let himself stare at her, at the way her pale hair fell along her soft cheek. At the little half smile on her pretty mouth.

He jerked his eyes away the moment she looked up at him. "Uh, where's Polly?" he asked.

"Amelia's father picked her up about a half an hour ago."

He dared to look at her again. She was smoothing her hair, guiding it away from her cheek and behind an ear.

"That's right," he said, sounding offhand and casual, though he felt anything but. "Didn't you tell me she was staying overnight?"

Jenny laughed. "That's right. And there's the party. Did I mention the party?"

"I think so."

"Polly's first boy-girl party. Can you believe it?"

Polly's *gone* for the day, he kept thinking. Except for the fuzz ball, Jen and I are alone.

In spite of the way his blood was suddenly roaring through his veins, he managed to keep up the chitchat. "I'd swear I saw her in diapers only yesterday."

Jen nodded and her eyes went tender. "You're right. She was a baby just yesterday. I'm sure of it, too."

They looked at each other, remembering. Or at least, Jen was probably remembering. Nick had other concerns: like how to stretch out his visit.

Then Jen said, "Listen. Have you had lunch? I was just about to make a sandwich."

"Lunch. Yeah. Sounds great." And good for an hour, at the very least.

She turned to the sink, flipped the faucet on and started washing her hands.

He suggested, "You got any of that smoked turkey?"

"—with lettuce and tomatoes."

He grinned. "And don't forget the ketchup."

She pretended to shudder. "Ugh. Ketchup." She always teased him about the ketchup.

And he always said, "Hey. I love ketchup. Lay it on good and thick."

She dried her hands, went to the fridge and pulled it open. Then she just stood there, staring at the inside of the refrigerator door, where three shelves held jars of pickles and mustard and green olives and jam—as well as a big plastic bottle full of the ketchup he loved.

"Andrew loved mayonnaise," she said, out of nowhere. She looked so sad, standing there, looking at all those bottles and jars. Sad and lost.

Nick experienced four distinct urges at once: to reach out, gather her close and offer her comfort. To grab her and shake her and shout, Andy's dead! To turn around and walk out of there and never come back. And to turn around and walk out of there and come back on Monday—when Polly would be there and Jen would be safe from the things he was probably going to try to do to her today.

He gratified none of those urges, only said gently, "Yeah, he did. He was nuts for the stuff."

"I don't keep mayonnaise in my house anymore." She said that defiantly, lifting her chin at him.

"Hey. If I ever want some, I'll bring it over my-self."

She let out another odd laugh, a slightly frantic one this time. "You don't even *like* mayonnaise."

"So we don't have a problem, do we?"

She made no reply, only stared at him.

He couldn't stand that stare. He took the two steps that brought him to her side. She let out a small gasp and fell back a fraction. He knew then for certain that she wanted him, too.

He knew it all. That she was fighting it. But that she would give in to it, if only he could manage to keep from handing her another reason to send him away.

The urge came on him again, very powerfully this time, to haul her against him and lower his mouth to hers.

But he sensed it was just a little too soon for that. So he grabbed the ketchup from its space in the door, took her slim hand and wrapped her fingers around the neck of the bottle.

She stared at him, stricken. Those shoulders of hers, which were wide for a woman, slumped just a little. His hand still covered hers. It felt soft and so good, warm over the cold neck of the bottle. He didn't want to let go.

But he did let go. He turned and opened the meat drawer, took out the turkey, then bent and opened one of the two lower drawers. A half head of lettuce and a lone tomato waited there. He scooped them up, nudged the door shut and put everything on the counter next to the sink.

She had watched the whole process, clutching the

ketchup bottle, her lips pressed together as if any second she might burst into tears.

He knew what she was waiting for. He knew her that well. She expected him to say, What's wrong? Or, Look, do you want me to go?

But damned if he would play the role of understanding friend for her today. He'd played that role for four long years, done a bang-up job of it, too. Even enjoyed it. Felt right about it. Felt good.

But not today. No, thanks.

"Do you want me to make my own sandwich?" he asked quietly.

She seemed to shake herself, and forced a smile. "No. Of course not. I'll do it."

"Great." He turned and left the kitchen without glancing back, giving her a moment to pull herself together, to make up a few lies to tell herself, about how nothing was going on here, about how Nick was her *friend*.

There was a smoke alarm and a 9-volt battery sitting on the table. He hooked the battery up and tucked it inside the alarm. Then he looked through the kitchen doorway. Jen had her back to him, busy making sandwiches. Her shoulders seemed a little straighter, he thought. She turned to reach for a knife. He caught a glimpse of her profile. Her mouth looked soft, her jaw relaxed.

Good.

"You want me to put this thing back on the wall?" He held up the alarm.

She looked over her shoulder. "Oh. Did you get the battery in?" He turned it around, so that she could see it. "That's great. It goes in the hall, over the guest bedroom door."

"Gotcha." He pressed the tester button. The thing gave a long, piercing beep. "Works fine."

"Good. Thanks." She turned back to the sandwiches.

She already had a stepladder set up in the hall. He climbed up the three steps and slid the device onto the mounting plate, stuck in the anchoring pin, then got down and folded up the ladder and put it in the hall closet, where he knew she always kept it.

When he returned to the dining room, she was putting down place mats and napkins. "Want milk?" she asked, sending him a bright smile.

"I'll get it." He went into the kitchen, washed his hands and got down the glasses. "How 'bout you?"

"Milk's fine," she told him.

So he poured the milk, thinking how well he knew her. How well he knew all the little things, like where she kept the milk glasses and the stepladder. He could go around her house blindfolded and still be able to find just about anything he needed.

He liked that. To really *know* the woman he wanted. Know the big, difficult things, like she still carried a torch for the husband she'd lost. And to know so many little things, too.

Always before, the women he'd wanted had started out as total strangers to him. In fact, the more exotic and different a woman was, the more attraction she seemed to have for him.

Now, with Jen, the thrill seemed to be, at least partly, in her familiarity. There seemed to be such a potential for…intimacy in that. That she knew him so well. That he knew her. That they'd been through so much together.

Intimacy. It was one of those words that Polly liked to throw around, one of those words he always teased her about—because deep down, he wanted some of that, some *intimacy*. He wanted a woman he could really talk to. A woman who really knew him. A woman *he* really knew.

"Ready?" Jen was standing at his side, holding a plate in each hand.

"You bet."

Nick put the milk back in the fridge and picked up the two full glasses. He followed Jen to the table. They sat down together, ate their sandwiches and drank their milk.

As they ate, Jen talked about her job and he talked about his. They laughed together some more, about Polly and the boy-girl party she insisted was just no big deal.

The whole time, Nick kept thinking that he probably ought to tell Jen about Sasha—if not specifically what had happened at the Nine-Seventeen Club, at least the basic fact that he'd had a change of heart about her. He also wanted to ask about the man who'd walked Jen to her door the night before.

But if he asked about that man, he'd have to explain how he'd seen him—that he'd been lurking down the street, hiding in the shadows. It wouldn't sound so good.

In fact, he felt almost certain that if he brought up what he'd seen, the two of them would end up arguing again—and Jen would have her excuse to send him away.

He had the same feeling of certainty when it came to mentioning the truth about Sasha. Jenny might not get angry with him over that. But as soon as he told her, she'd start looking for reasons that he ought to leave.

Well, he didn't want to leave.

He wanted his chance to get what he'd just realized he was after.

He wanted some time to make Jen admit she now saw him as more than a friend.

But he had to go easy. He had to take the day kind of slow, keep it light, keep it harmless. At least for the next few hours.

Jenny felt warm all over. Light as air. Giddy as a schoolgirl.

The day just seemed brighter, somehow, now that Nick was here. Maybe it was a little dangerous—to her peace of mind, if nothing else—to let herself be alone with him this way when she still had all these thoroughly inappropriate feelings for him. But it was just so *good* to see him. And it was also good to know that the incident of Thursday night no longer hung like a dark cloud over their friendship, that he wanted to forget about it every bit as much as she did.

Of course, she really did have to watch herself. Her emotions were just a little bit unstable today. Somehow, the simple act of Nick's pressing a ketchup bottle into her hand had nearly undone her. She had to keep herself from overreacting in that way again.

Nick *was* her friend. And until this silly crush she had on him finally faded, she would just have to get used to keeping rein on her emotions when he was around. Either that, or avoid him all the time.

And avoidance was not something you did to a friend.

When they'd finished their sandwiches, they carried their plates and glasses back to the sink and put them into the dishwasher.

Then Nick asked, "Okay, what other projects besides that smoke alarm have you been putting off asking me to handle?"

So she went ahead and showed him the light fixture over the hall bathroom's sink that had to be completely dismantled before the darn bulb could be changed. He took it apart in two minutes flat. She handed him the bulb and he put it all back together. Then there was the stove burner that had stopped working. That took an hour, but he fixed it for her. And the leak in the faucet in her own bathroom. For that, he found a spare washer in the jumbled pile of nuts and bolts out in Andrew's junk drawer in the garage.

By the time he finished playing handyman, it was almost five. She told him regretfully that she really had to head over to Raley's and get the week's grocery shopping done.

He put on one of his pitiful looks. "Hey, don't I get dinner? For a smoke alarm, a light fixture, a leaky faucet and a bad burner, I think I ought to get a free meal, at least."

She tried to be firm. "I gave you lunch."

"I want more than lunch."

"I gathered. But you've had a lot of free meals around here lately."

"All those dinners don't count."

"Oh, really? Why not?"

"Because *I* said they don't."

She shook her head and sighed in exasperation, but he only went on looking at her as if he'd be crushed if she told him no.

"Come on, Jen. *Please.*"

What could she say?

Before she could open her mouth to give in, he came up with another suggestion. "I've got it. Why don't *I* cook *you* dinner for a change? And don't look at me like that. I'll have you know I make a mean veal piccata. We'll go on over to Raley's, and I'll get what I need while you buy your own groceries. We'll come back here, you can unload your stuff, we'll pick up the fuzz ball—and go to my place."

He looked thoroughly pleased with himself.

Hmm, she thought. To have *him* cook, at *his* place. A definite change of pace. And it did sound like fun. Maybe too *much* fun.

"Look," he said. "It would be good for both of us. I'm free for the evening, and Polly's at Amelia's. You might as well get out of the house. What harm can it do?"

What harm? she thought, a little shiver of anticipation slinking naughtily down her spine.

Oh, she was just a silly fool. Nick had no idea of her secret crush. He was in love with that Sasha woman and only thought of Jenny as a friend. It wasn't as if she had to worry about him trying to make a pass at her or anything.

Again, the incident with the ketchup bottle flitted through her mind. The way he'd so deliberately taken her hand and put the ketchup in it. The strange light in his eyes right then.

The fact that she had been upset, and over something just a little bit ridiculous: that Andrew had loved mayonnaise and now she had none in her house. And that Nick adored ketchup and what would happen if she lost Nick, too? Would she stop buying ketchup? Would she open the refrigerator door and find *neither* mayonnaise *nor* ketchup waiting there?

All right, it had been a stupid thing to want to cry over. But she *had* felt like crying. And she'd waited for Nick to ask her what was wrong, which he normally would have done.

But he hadn't. He hadn't asked her.

Why hadn't he asked her?

It was just totally unlike him, not to mutter a soft, "Hey," not to pull her close and rub her back and—

Oh, it was all way too confusing. She was making mountains out of dust specks.

They were both a little lonely. And he wanted to spend a pleasant evening with a friend. He had it right. There really couldn't be any harm to it.

"So, what do you say?" he asked.

She gave him a bright smile. "I say yes."

Chapter Twelve

They ended up cooking together in Nick's huge gourmet kitchen while Daisy batted a stuffed catnip mouse around on the gleaming marble floor. Nick handled the veal and the garlic bread, Jenny took care of the linguine and the tossed green salad. They'd bought two bottles of Soave to go with the food, though Nick had insisted that if she wanted Chenin Blanc, she should have Chenin Blanc. They didn't have to have Italian wine to go with their Italian meal.

"Soave is fine," she'd told him and reached for a second bottle—then put it back on the shelf without laying it in the cart. "I suppose we really don't need two."

"The hell we don't." He grabbed that second bottle and set it in the cart.

So they had one bottle of wine with the meal—and

another that they carried into the living room afterward. Jenny shucked off her shoes and sat on the sofa. Nick lit the fire—a very simple process, he just turned a knob. And he put on some music: Celine Dion.

When that gorgeous, lush voice filled every corner of the giant room, he turned and looked at her. "Polly's suggestion, remember?"

She sipped her Soave and suppressed a smile. "Mmm-hmm."

"Supposed to impress the women."

"Do I look impressed?"

"No. You look like you're trying not to laugh, if you want to know the truth."

She sipped some more and glanced at the one-handed clock built into the slate wall above the fire. It was after nine. She probably ought to ask Nick to take her home.

And she would. Soon. But not right yet. They'd shared such a lovely afternoon and evening. She just didn't want it to end.

She teased, "Well, maybe you should play something that's a little more *you*. After all, I really don't need impressing, anyway."

He pretended to look crestfallen. "You don't?"

"You know I don't." She said that quickly, thinking that what they were doing felt very much like flirting.

But, no. It wasn't. It was just...fooling around. A little harmless teasing, that was all.

He said, "But you were impressed, weren't you, with the veal?"

"You think I had two helpings to be polite?"

"It was great, wasn't it?"

"Yes. In fact, from now on I'm not going to feel

the least bit sorry for you when you're hanging around my house at dinnertime. Now I know it's all an act, that you can cook a terrific meal all by yourself.''

''Only veal,'' he protested. ''And you made the salad and fixed the pasta.''

''You could have done it all.''

''Damn. You're on to me.''

They shared a smile. Jenny thought that it was a lovely moment, with the fire dancing in the fireplace and Daisy curled up on a chair nearby.

Maybe too lovely a moment...

He said, ''So. Nix on the Celine Dion?''

She nodded. ''It's beautiful, but how about some Rolling Stones or something?''

He shook his head. ''Not on a full stomach. Not at *our* age.''

''The Rolling Stones are a lot older than we are.''

''Jen. Listen to me. No Rolling Stones. Not tonight.''

She almost asked, Why not tonight? But she didn't. It seemed kind of a dangerous question, for some silly reason.

She set her glass down and padded over in her stocking feet to join him at the CD rack. They spent several minutes debating the options and finally, between them, chose some easy listening and a little bit of country and even some soft rock. Nick put the CDs in a cartridge and music filled the room again.

They sat, together this time, on the long black leather sofa. Nick picked up the wine bottle from the big black-lacquer coffee table in front of them. He filled his own glass, then raised the bottle toward her. ''More?''

She probably should have said, No thanks, I ought to get on home. But she didn't say it. After all, hadn't she just helped him choose the music? It seemed only right that she stay and listen a while.

She nodded and held out her glass. He leaned a little closer to her, preparing to pour.

The scent of him came to her. Yes. She did know his scent. A scent for which she had no words. It was just *his* scent. Nick's. Real and immediate to her—just as Andrew's scent had been lost somewhere, had become only words now.

But Nick's scent.

It was a scent that she had known for years without ever acknowledging, even to herself, that she knew it. A scent that had at first meant adversary, and then friend.

And now...

She hesitated, not sure of what word she sought, the word that meant his scent now aroused her, reminded her poignantly that she was a woman and he was a man.

What was the word for that scent that had no words: lover?

Denial rose up again.

No. Nick was not her lover. How dangerous for her to even let herself think such a word.

The wine tumbled out of the bottle and into her glass, slightly golden, thin and pure.

''That's enough,'' she said.

Nick tilted the bottle up, stopping the flow. One tiny drop quivered on the rim, then fell at last, disappearing instantly, creating hardly a ripple.

Jenny looked up to find Nick watching her, the bottle still poised.

She thought, I'm leaving now. I'm going to tell him it's time for me to go home.

But she didn't tell him. She said nothing.

Nick set the wine bottle down.

Somehow, though she knew that she ought to look away, she didn't. Couldn't. His dark eyes mesmerized her. Looking into them made her whole body melt and burn. Such a lovely feeling.

A feeling lost to her for too many years now. The feeling of melting. Of heat and hollowing out, awakened by a man's eyes.

He kept on looking at her. He would not look away. His eyes kept working on her, sending heat and yearning pulsing all through her.

He lifted a hand. She didn't move, only stayed with him, where she wanted to be. With his eyes that wouldn't let go of her, his eyes that drew on her, making her breasts feel hard and hungry for caresses, the nipples turning to tight, sensitive buds. Making that tugging, blooming sensation low in her belly. That waiting, anticipatory feeling—the longing of a woman for the touch of a certain man.

He took her glass. She hadn't even sipped from it. Took it and set it down, somewhere near his glass and the nearly empty bottle of wine. She didn't know where he set it exactly, because she couldn't look there.

She couldn't look anywhere. But into Nick's eyes.

He touched her face, cupping her chin in his big, slightly rough hand. She could smell lemon, from the slices he had cut to cook with the veal. Sharp and clean, that lemon smell.

Lemon. And the scent of him, for which there were no words.

Somewhere far away, the music they had chosen together played on. But the music seemed unreal, like the big room with its expanse of marble floor. Like the sleeping kitten on the black chair. Like the one-handed clock on the wall that had warned her it was time to go home.

Jenny sighed, and a small shudder went through her. Nick felt that shudder. He *had* to feel it, since his hand still cupped her chin. He had to see it with those dark, demanding eyes.

Warned. She had been warned. By the one-handed clock. By her own wiser self.

But she had not heeded the warnings. She'd been too busy, getting herself into this situation. She had shucked off her shoes and said yes to more wine, wandered over to the CD rack to choose what music they'd play.

And now it was too late. Now she would have what she wanted, though it was wrong. Though there was some woman named Sasha.

And the memory of Andrew, of his death. Of the pain she had sworn to herself she'd never have to feel again.

Nick's eyes came closer. They blotted out what was left of the world.

His mouth touched hers, so lightly. It was soft, that mouth, and tender. He brushed it, back and forth, against her own. Something rose in her throat—a whimper of need.

His arms went around her and his mouth opened on hers.

No, she thought. Don't do this. Don't make me do this.

But his mouth was on hers, his scent surrounded her, his tongue delved in.

Andrew, she thought. You left me and I swore.

I swore never. Never again. Standing there at your grave—how long? A few months after you left me. Staring at the beautiful headstone that we chose together, Nick and I.

Your name there on that headstone: Andrew Jonas Brown. And the dates of your birth and death.

And at the bottom: Husband Father Son Friend.

I stood there at your grave and I swore I would never, ever again...

And the robin. There had been a robin. Clearly male, the breast such a deep orange it really did look red. The robin appeared out of nowhere, or that was how it seemed. He flew down out of the sky and perched on the stone bench a few feet away, that red breast puffed up, knowing eyes small and sharp and seeing everything.

He sang for me, that robin.

I remember, Andrew. I remember how it was....

Nick's hand, on the buttons of her shirt, moving down, so swift and sure, taking her clothes away. All of them. Gone away. Even her thick white socks, which he peeled off slowly, one at a time. She watched them falling to the marble floor, leaving her with nothing.

No protection from his touch.

From her need.

From the promise she was breaking.

The dark head moved down. She cradled it as he captured her breast, suckled it, made her arch her body up, hungry, needful, wanting more.

Nick pulled back. She thought, yes, now—I'll turn away. I'll end this, I will, before—

But his eyes found her. His eyes wouldn't let her go. He took her hands and guided them to the sides of his shirt. And then she was taking that shirt, pulling it up, and over his head. Her heart beat hollow and hard beneath her bare breasts and her blood moved through her veins thickly, oh so sweetly...

She undressed him. She revealed his body, which was so hard and big, the arms and legs heavy with muscle, the bones sturdy and strong. Dark, crisp hair curled on his chest and between his powerful thighs, where the proof of his desire for her stood up proud and sure.

Sitting on the sofa, with him standing above her, she touched him. And he groaned. She took that groan into herself, as she would soon take him. All of him, inside of her, filling the burning, needful hollow at the center of herself.

She looked up. His eyes waited, caught her, wouldn't let her go.

And she took him. Into her mouth. She tasted him, the whole hard length of him. She stroked him with her lips and tongue.

He didn't let her do that for long. He put his hand behind her head, curled his strong fingers in her hair and made her look at him again. His hand slid down, caressing her shoulder, brushing along her arm. His fingers twined with hers.

He gave a tug. She needed no more urging. She stood. He reached for her.

Another kiss, a naked kiss. His body branding itself all along hers, the strength and power of it making her shudder again, her breasts pushing against him, her sex rubbing his.

He lifted his head.

She got out two words. "We shouldn't—"

And then his cruel, wonderful mouth took the words away. He drank them into himself as his tongue toyed with hers, until she forgot them, until it was as if they had never been said.

When that kiss was through, he took her hand once more. He turned, pulling her, stumbling a little, behind him. They crossed the marble floor. It was warm, that floor. Heating elements ran beneath it, little thin lines, like wires. Nick had explained it all to her, the first time he brought her and Polly here to show her his new house, right after he moved in.

Polly.

Her daughter's name burst into her mind. Polly— off at her first boy-girl party on this night when she, herself, was here with Nick, naked.

"Mom, it's good that you're dating," Polly had said. "But you're going to have to get past this *friend* thing, you really are...."

Oh, Polly, am I past it yet? she thought with a tiny laugh that came out like a cry.

Nick stopped when she let out that cry. They were halfway down the long hall that led to his bedroom. He stopped and turned to her. He took her face in his big hands. And he kissed her again, long and slow and deep, so she forgot everything but how much she wanted him.

Forgot everything but his touch. His maleness. His scent.

The scent of a lover.

Yes. Lover. The right word, after all.

He stroked her bare shoulders, ran his hands down her back. She knew his male purpose: to make her forget her own frantic cry. And she helped him, she colluded with him, pushing her mouth up to his, rubbing her breasts against his chest.

When all she could think of once again was her hunger, he released her enough to pull her the rest of the way to his room. The lights were already on in there, recessed lights, built into the ceiling, tucked away in the high walls. They made soft pools on the floor, on the wide bed with its black silk coverlet, on the black, thick pillows and the pale birchwood bureaus.

He led her to the bed and guided her down on it, his mouth finding hers again, his powerful body pressing her into the black silk. For one moment he left her, to take a small box from the nightstand, to slide a condom in place.

Then he was with her again, stroking her, kissing her, touching all her secret places, delving into them, opening them. He moved down her body, until his mouth found the heart of her. She opened for him without a murmur of protest. She rose, shameless, toward that incredible, forbidden kiss.

She shattered, with his dark head between her thighs.

As the aftershocks trembled through her, he rose up.

His hands found her hands, his fingers lacing into hers. He lifted her hands, over her head, spread them wide on the pile of black pillows. He held them there as he penetrated her, slowly, deeply, his eyes looking into hers, holding her there.

She cried out again. Just a woman's cry, this time. No anguish or doubt in it. No hesitation. Simply a deep emptiness, filled.

She moved with him, rising to meet each stroke, falling back only to rise again, sighing, thinking yes, yes, yes. Another sigh. And yes, again....

Fulfillment poured through her, a shower of light, an endless expansion within a series of contractions.

She heard him moan as he found release, too.

When it was over, she lay beneath him, still joined to him, feeling as if she floated on some endless, warm sea.

But finally, thought came back to her. Doubt began to rise.

She moved, tried to push at him.

He lifted on those muscled forearms, looked down at her.

She thought, *No, I won't look at you. I won't—*

He took her chin in his hand. Held her there, for his eyes.

And then his mouth came down. That wonderful mouth.

How, after tonight, would she look at that mouth again, without thinking, *Please kiss me? Please touch me. Please make love to me....*

His mouth worked its magic. She sighed, lifted her arms to pull him even closer. Down where they were still joined, she could feel him rising once more.

* * *

They fell asleep some time after two.

Nick woke before dawn, knew a moment of complete disorientation, a certainty that what had happened had only been a dream.

But then he turned his head on the pillow. She was there, in his bed with him: Jen.

She lay on her back, her eyes closed, the covers up to her chin.

He rolled toward her, took the edge of the black silk comforter and slowly, carefully, pulled it away.

At first, she didn't wake. So he indulged himself in the pleasure of looking at her. At her pale skin and light hair spread on the black pillow. At the fine, wide shoulders, the full breasts he had kissed. At the faint, thin lines of stretch marks on her belly; they seemed beautiful to him somehow, because he knew how she'd got them: having Polly.

His gaze wandered lower, to the pretty golden curls between her long, smooth legs. He wanted to touch those curls again, to feel their softness, to burrow into them and find the satiny slick female heart of her beneath.

She would be wet for him. Open for him.

Whatever happened later, they would both know that. They would both remember what they had done together, here, tonight. That whatever her hesitations, she had given herself completely in the end. She had reached for him, touched him, helped him to undress. Taken him willingly into herself.

She stirred and opened those blue eyes, started to speak. He put his hand over her mouth.

"Shh," he said. He didn't want any talking. Not now. Not till the light of day, at least.

He knew exactly what he'd done that night: seduced her. Seduced Jen.

And he knew that when the talking started, there could very well be hell to pay.

So, all right. He would pay. But not yet. Not while the smallest fraction of the night remained. Tonight was his. *Jen* was his. For as long as he could keep words and daylight at bay.

And after that?

Would he lose her friendship over this?

And what would his life be like, without Jen as his friend?

He shook his head, as another warning to her not to speak—and also as a caution to himself that it was better not to think now of what might happen when daylight came. Better not to waste a moment of this— of him and Jen, naked in his bed.

He took his hand away. She continued to watch him, blue eyes wary, strong chin thrust out a little, waiting to see what he planned to do.

So he lowered his mouth to hers and claimed her again.

Chapter Thirteen

Jenny woke to a rumbling sound. She slid her hand out from beneath the covers, groping toward that rumble. Her hand encountered a small, warm body covered with fur: Daisy. Little Daisy was sharing her pillow with her. And the sun—the sun was shining through the half-open blinds over the glass doors that led out to the patio off Nick's bedroom.

She turned her head, saw Nick there beside her and thought of the night before.

No. Never mind that.

She looked the other way again, back toward the fluffy body of the purring kitten. Beyond the kitten, the clock on the nightstand chided her: almost nine.

She had to get home, get a shower. Pick Polly up by eleven.

There was plenty of time, really. She knew that. But she felt such urgency. To get out of there, to get home.

She pushed back the covers and jumped from the bed. The kitten sat up, stretched and yawned, then flopped back down and began washing a rear leg.

Jenny looked at herself. Naked. She was naked.

It shouldn't have shocked her. She remembered very well that she'd been naked for a good part of the night before. But still, it did startle her. It reminded her too forcefully that everything she remembered had actually taken place.

She glanced back at the man on the bed: still sleeping. And her clothes were all the way out in the living room, for heaven's sake.

She had to get them on and then wake him, ask him to drive her home. Oh, why hadn't she had sense enough to bring her own car? Then she wouldn't have to wake him, wouldn't have to face him—at least not right now, when she had to get home, get cleaned up, collect her daughter from all the way across town.

She turned for the door to the hall. Lord, it was a long hall, she thought as she strode down it, almost running, her breasts bouncing in an undignified manner, only longing to get to the end of it and get some clothes on.

In the living room, the fire still danced along those logs that never burned. The half-empty bottle of wine sat on the black-lacquer coffee table, next to two full glasses. Strewn on the floor in front of the sofa and under the coffee table, were her clothes and Nick's. The room looked like just what it was: the scene of a recent seduction.

A seduction.

Yes. Nick had seduced her.

What had happened was all his fault.

But even as she thought those words, she knew they weren't honest. They were part of the truth, perhaps. But not the whole truth.

If Nick had seduced her, he hadn't done it alone.

She had helped him. Conspired with him to create the perfect opportunity for it to happen—after a lovely day together, after a beautiful dinner, with the help of a couple of bottles of nice wine, to the accompaniment of a cartridge full of music they had chosen together.

Jenny glanced from the fire to the bottle and glasses on the coffee table and then to the tangled clothing on the floor. Well, at least the music she had helped to choose didn't play on. Sometime in the night, the thing had switched itself off.

"Get dressed," she said to herself and the huge, silent room. "Get your clothes on and then march back to that bedroom and tell Nick you have to go."

She strode to the coffee table and crouched down, yanking her clothes from under there, getting them free of Nick's. She had her bra and panties on and was zipping up her jeans when he spoke from behind her.

"Jen."

She knew she had to face him, had to look in those dark eyes. But she couldn't bear to do it with her jeans unzipped and her shirt off. Swiftly she yanked up the zipper, pressed the top snap shut. Then she grabbed for her shirt, pulled it on and made herself turn as she buttoned it up.

He stood in the wide entrance to the long hall. With some relief she saw that he'd pulled on a pair of Levi's and a long-sleeved shirt before he came looking for her. He hadn't bothered much with buttons, however. The top button of his Levi's remained undone. And his powerful chest with its mat of dark, curly hair confronted her between the open sides of the shirt. He looked so…aggressively male, standing there with his shirt open and his feet bare. Or at least, that was her initial impression.

But then she looked up, into his eyes. She saw tenderness and real concern.

Her throat closed. She felt the silly tears rising.

She bit them back, pressed them down. All at once, she wanted to shout at him. To leap across the marble floor between them and pound on that hairy chest, to scream, Don't look at me like that, with those caring eyes. Not after what you did—what *we* did—last night!

But no. She would not do that. She would not scream and shout and act like some wild woman. What had happened had happened. And she had to be on her way.

She told him just that in a tight, brisk voice. "Listen, I really have to get going. I have to pick Polly up, over in Greenhaven."

He said nothing, only stood there, with his caring eyes and his unbuttoned shirt.

She dropped to the edge of the couch, picked up a sock and pulled it on her right foot. She grabbed for the other sock, pausing before yanking it on to glance over at him. He was still just standing there, watching her. "Please, Nick. Really. Will you put on some shoes and drive me home?"

He came toward her then, striding silently on those bare feet. She wanted to shout again, Stop! Don't come any closer.…

But of course, she didn't. She merely jerked on her sock and grabbed for a shoe.

He had reached her side. She could see him there, out of the corner of her eye, see his powerful legs in worn denim, feel the warmth his body gave off.

She spoke to his bare feet. "Could you just...please put your shoes on?"

He dropped to a crouch before her—and took her tennis shoe from her suddenly limp hand. "Jen. Come on. Will you look at me, at least?"

"Just give me my shoe."

"Jen."

"My shoe, damn you! Give it to me!" She actually shouted the words, so loud that poor little Daisy, who'd appeared from the hall, arched up her back, hissed and danced sideways until she ran into the wall. Then she whirled and bolted off the way she had come.

Dead silence—during which he did not hand over her shoe.

Finally, he whispered, "Look at me, Jen."

She didn't want to, she sincerely did not. But she did. She raised her eyes. They locked with his.

She fisted her hands—to keep them from hitting him. She longed to shout some more, to demand, Is this what my daughter taught you? All this kindness and concern? Did she tell you to be so *sensitive* and *caring* the morning after?

"We have to talk about this," he said, very gently.

She spoke through clenched teeth. "No, we do not. It was a mistake—"

"It wasn't."

"It *was*. A mistake. It never should have happened. And I'm sorry it happened."

"I'm not."

"Well. You should be."

He tried to reach out. She flinched. "Don't. Please. Don't." She stood, backed away from him, between the couch and the big coffee table, stopping when she'd reached the far end.

He rose then, too, still holding her shoe. "Come on, Jen." He looked so hurt, so bewildered.

How could he look like that? How could he stand there, holding her shoe and looking at her as if she was the one who'd done wrong here?

Even if she *had* done wrong. At least she was willing to let it go. At least she was willing to—

He cut into her thoughts. "Jen, I realized something yesterday, something I think I've been hiding from myself for months now. I realized—"

She threw up a hand. "Stop. No. This is…insane. There is nothing to discuss, the way I see it. Right now, I'm, well, I'm fed up with you. And disgusted with myself. You never should have kissed me. I never should have kissed you back. And we certainly shouldn't have allowed ourselves to end up in bed together."

"Why not?"

She gaped at him, then echoed in disbelief, "Why *not?*"

"Yeah." His eyes had turned harder. They sparked with dark fire. "Why the hell not?"

"Boy, you have got a short memory, mister."

"I asked you, Jen. Why the hell not?"

"In a word, Sasha. You do remember Sasha, don't you? The one you're so in love with. The one you had to have my daughter *training* you for?"

His anger had risen to keep pace with hers. He glowered at her. "Look. Forget Sasha."

She let out a harsh laugh. "Forget Sasha? Just like that?"

"Right. Forget her. Just like that. I saw her night before last in the Nine-Seventeen Club. She was hanging all over some big, buff low-class guy just like me. And I felt relief. That's all. Relief that I can quit telling myself I love her when I don't even know her—and I don't *want* to know her."

At that news, Jenny felt as if something had cut off her air. She sucked in a big, hard breath. "You don't…love Sasha?"

"Hell, no. I never did. I realize that now."

"But…if you don't love Sasha, if you *knew* that you didn't love Sasha, then why didn't you tell me yesterday? Why didn't you say something, at least before…what happened last night?"

"Because I *wanted* yesterday, damn it. I wanted last night. I wanted to be with you. And I guess I knew that as long as you thought I had a thing for someone else, you'd let down your guard a little, let me get close to you."

There it was again, that feeling that she wasn't getting air. She couldn't believe it, that he could know her so well, that he could understand so completely how her mind worked, the kind of lies she was willing to tell herself. It stunned her. No one had ever known her that well.

Except Andrew.

Her knees felt wobbly. She sank to the sofa. Nick sat, too, at the other end.

She accused in a hollow voice, "So you tricked me."

He looked down at the shoe he held in his hand, and then back at her. "Jen. I don't think you did anything you didn't want to do."

It was true, of course. Way too true. No matter how hard she kept trying to blame him, she *couldn't* blame him. Not when so much of the blame actually belonged to her.

Oh, there was just no point in talking about this. She had to get home.

"Look. May I please have my shoe, now?"

With a weary exhalation of breath, he bent down, picked up her other shoe, then handed them both to her. She could feel his eyes on her as she pulled them on and tied the laces.

"Now," she said, when she had all her clothes on at last. "I really have to go."

"What time do you have to get Polly?"

"Nick—"

"What time."

Grudgingly, she confessed, "Eleven."

"So maybe you can spare me a few more minutes here."

"Nick, there's just no reason to—"

"Can you spare me a few damn minutes, or not?"

She closed her eyes and rubbed them with her fingertips. "All right. If you insist."

"Yeah. Okay. I *insist*."

"You don't have to become sarcastic."

"And you don't have to go into your snow queen routine."

Snow queen. He used to call her that, years and

years ago, behind her back. To Andrew. She'd heard him say it once or twice. "If the snow queen will let you, how 'bout we get a beer?" Or, "Hell, bud, you got to check with the snow queen on everything, now?"

Oh, why were they doing this? She only wanted to go home.

He said, "Look. Can we just talk about Andy? Can we just talk about why you think you have to spend the rest of your life married to a ghost?"

She closed her eyes again, dragged in a breath. "I do not think I have to spend the rest of my life married to a ghost. I don't want to be married to *anyone*. I just want..." She couldn't find the words.

And he wouldn't wait for her to find them. "What? *What* do you want?"

She stared at him hopelessly.

He swore.

She shook her head. "Won't you please take me home?"

She was a tall woman, but to Nick right then, she looked very small and lost, sitting there at the other end of his sofa in her wrinkled shirt, with her shoulders hunched over, as if he'd been beating on them. He felt like a heel.

All those articles Polly had made him read said a man needed to talk to a woman, to *communicate* with her, to really listen when she told him her feelings and her needs.

Well, how the hell was a guy supposed to listen if a woman *wouldn't* talk?

The articles had never said a damn thing about that.

He was out of his depth here, and he knew it. In way, way over his head.

And he'd probably blown everything anyway by making love to her last night. Probably all those articles had just assumed he'd have sense enough to get the talking done *before* he attempted anything so dangerous as sex.

A powerful yearning came over him: for his old self, for the man who wanted nothing more from a woman than a few laughs and good, clean fun between the sheets. Things had been so much simpler then. Sex hadn't been dangerous then.

Shoulders still hunched and head hanging down, Jen glanced over at him. Her blue eyes held a world of misery and silent appeal.

He gave in to her. "All right. Fine. I'll take you home."

She didn't say a word on the whole drive to her house.

One of the neighbor kids had left a red wagon in her driveway, so he swung around and pulled up under the branches of the mulberry tree.

When he shut off the engine, she turned to him, gave him a sad little smile and a deep, tired sigh.

He'd already decided not to push things any further right then. "Hey. It's all right." It wasn't, but it seemed like the right thing to say. "Take some time. I'll call you."

"About Monday, I..."

Monday. Tomorrow. He'd forgotten. Polly would be expecting him. "I'll call you tonight, okay?"

She stiffened. He got the message. If he was giving

her that "time" he'd promised, then tonight was way too soon for him to be calling her. "Jen. We have to at least decide what to tell Polly."

She nodded. "Okay. Tonight, then. Give me a call."

He wanted to touch her, but somehow he didn't dare, so he just reached across her and opened her door.

She gave him one last, pained smile. "Bye." And then she slid from the car and ran across the lawn, under the mulberry tree, up to her front step.

He watched her fumble with the key and let herself in. She never once turned back to glance his way, only stepped over the threshold and shut the door against him.

He knew he should go. There was no point in sitting out there on the street, hating himself, trying not to be mad at her for refusing to talk to him, feeling grim and sad and wondering how he was ever going to get through to her.

Yeah, he knew he should go. But he didn't go. Right then, he didn't have the initiative to do a damn thing.

Which was why he was still parked in front of the house, staring blindly out his windshield, when Jen's garage door went rumbling up. He turned in his seat at the sound.

He saw Jen's car shoot out, rear end first, moving way too fast.

She must have seen the little red wagon at the last minute, because she swerved wildly to avoid it. The rear of the car swung way to the left and picked up speed. It hit the lawn and kept going.

It would have run right off the lawn and into Nick's car—except for that big fruitless mulberry tree. Nick cringed and shut his eyes at the moment of impact. Metal hit ungiving wood, crunching and groaning.

When Nick looked again, the tree trunk appeared to have taken a big bite out of the back of Jen's car.

Chapter Fourteen

Nick shoved open his door, jumped out and sprinted across the lawn. When he got to her side, she was slumped over the steering wheel. She'd been a whole car length away from the point of impact, and the vehicle hadn't been going *that* fast. Still, for one endless, awful second, he was sure she had somehow been hurt.

He grabbed her door handle and yanked the thing open. "God. Jenny. I'm sorry. I didn't mean to—"

But then she lifted her head. No blood, no bruises. Nothing—except for the mute agony in her eyes. "I'm all right. Really." She raised her hands from the steering wheel and stared at them. "Look. Shaking. So stupid. They're shaking. I wasn't paying attention. Driving too fast. Too fast, I know it. Then I saw that wagon…" She put her hands back on the wheel and held on hard, as if by doing that she could make them stop shaking. "I have to get over to Amelia's. Right now. They've been trying to reach me since ten last night."

Oh God, he thought. Polly. Something's happened to Polly. He demanded, "What the hell is it? Is Polly okay?"

She let go of the wheel. "Yes." Then she shook her head. "No. Nick, I can't explain now. I have to go...."

He reached across her and pulled the keys from the ignition. "I'll drive you."

"No, really. I can drive. I can."

"Maybe you can. But this car's going nowhere. The rear end's caved in."

"But I—"

"Come on." He took her arm. She stared at him blankly for a moment. "Come on," he said again.

"All right." She grabbed her purse from the passenger seat and let him pull her out from behind the wheel. Once she was on her feet, she swayed and leaned against him. He worried again that she'd sustained some injury. She looked unharmed, but maybe...

"Are you sure you're not hurt?"

"No. No, I'm okay. Just...upset. Way too upset. And I have to go, Nick. I have to go now."

"All right. The car's right here." They started down the slight slope of the lawn, his arm over her shoulders. She leaned on him heavily. He didn't mind that at all. He only wished he knew for sure if Polly was all right.

But he'd get her in the car first, get going. And then he'd find out the whole story.

A neighbor woman came running up the sidewalk

just as he was settling Jen into the passenger seat of the Cadillac.

"What's happened? Jenny, are you okay?"

Jen gestured weakly with a wave of a hand. "I'm fine, really. Just careless."

"Oh, your poor car..."

"It's all right. I'll take care of it later. Right now—"

"We have to go," Nick finished for her as he shut her door.

"Is there anything I can *do?*"

He was already heading around to his side of the car. "No. Nothing. But thanks." He got in, buckled up. Jen watched him, a dazed look on her face. He tried a smile. "Better fasten your seat belt." Moving as if she were a woman in dream, she did. He turned the key and pulled away from the curb. As they drove off, in his rearview mirror, he saw the neighbor, staring after them, shaking her head.

He got them on the highway before he asked, "Greenhaven, right?"

"Right." She named an exit.

He dared to ask then, "Has Polly been hurt?"

Jen closed her eyes and leaned back in the seat. "No. It's not that, thank God."

He let out the breath he didn't even know he'd been holding. "Then what's happened?"

She sighed. "Oh, Nick..."

"Come on. Tell me."

At last, she started talking. "It's Amelia. Amelia's got a boyfriend. Her parents didn't know about him. Amelia never even mentioned him."

"Something happened with this boy, is that it?"

"Yes. Something happened. At the party. You remember the party?"

"Right. Last night."

Jen nodded. "The boy came to the party. He'd been drinking."

Nick swore under his breath and gripped the steering wheel tighter. "How old is this kid?"

"Sixteen, I think. Sixteen. And drinking. He took the girls for a ride in his car."

Nick swore again, more crudely than the first time.

Jen went on, her eyes still closed, her head on the backrest. "A highway patrolman pulled them over. They took the boy away. And the girls got a police escort home."

Nick swore for the third time. "Who is the boy? I'll kill him."

Jen sat up then. She opened her eyes and she stared at him squarely. "Nick. Don't. If you're going to get crazy about this, you'd better wait in the car when we get there."

He met her gaze, then looked back at the road. "I'm going in with you." He said the words firmly—and felt certain as he said them that she would say Polly wasn't his daughter, that she didn't want him involved.

But he was wrong. She only warned, "Not a word, then. Not a single word. You'll let me handle this myself."

It was better than he'd expected. He promised, "I swear. Not a word."

Amelia's parents, Will and Nancy Gordon, didn't seem the least surprised when Nick arrived with Jenny. But then again, they had lived next door to the Browns for a decade. They had known Nick as Andrew's friend—and they'd witnessed the way he'd stuck by Jenny and her daughter after Andrew's death. They probably didn't see it as the least bit odd that Nick would show up at a time like this.

And, Jenny realized, it wasn't odd, not at all. She only felt uncomfortable about it because of last night— because everything had changed between her and Nick now, and she still hadn't a clue as to how she was going to deal with that change.

But the Gordons, who knew nothing of the change, greeted Nick quietly and then launched into agonized apologies.

"Oh, Jenny, I'm so sorry," Nancy insisted. "We never would have let the girls out of our sight if we'd known. But we just had no clue Amelia was seeing *anyone*—let alone such a dangerous boy."

Will Gordon added darkly, "A boy she *won't* be seeing anymore."

Nancy looked as if she might cry. "She's only *thirteen*. We just never imagined she'd be seeing some older boy behind our backs..."

Jenny put her arm around Nancy. "Listen. Please don't think I'm blaming you for what happened. I'm not, not in the least."

"Thank you," said Will.

Nancy shook her head. "Amelia just hasn't been happy since we left the old house. She misses her old school. And Polly—Amelia's just lost without Polly, even though they're on the phone every day. But you know how they were."

Jenny did know. "Inseparable."

"Yes. Oh, I suppose I should have seen this coming,

or something *like* this. But I only kept thinking that I should give her time, that she would adjust.''

''What else could you have done?''

''Oh, I don't know. I just don't know....''

Guilt kept nagging at Jenny. After all, there was something *she* could have done: been home where she belonged last night when the trouble occurred. She spoke her guilt aloud, careful not to look at Nick, who stood a few feet away, near the entrance to the Gordons' living room. ''I'm just sorry I wasn't there, last night, when you tried to call.''

Nancy patted the hand Jenny had wrapped around her shoulder. ''We did try your cell phone.''

Guilt prodded harder. Jenny always carried that phone—just in case. But last night she'd left it in her purse on the counter in Nick's kitchen. And when the Gordons tried to reach her, she'd been in the bedroom, too far away to hear it ring. ''I'm...sorry,'' she said, her voice weak. Ineffectual.

Again, Nancy patted her hand. ''It was just a bad set of circumstances all the way around.''

Will said, ''Nancy and I have been talking this over. Amelia is going to be grounded for a while. And we think it might be best if we suspended phone privileges, too.''

Jenny nodded. ''I understand. I haven't really decided on the consequences for Polly yet. But you're probably right. It would be better if the girls don't talk on the phone or get together for a while.''

''Give them some time to deal with what they've done,'' Will added, ''without the opportunity to commiserate about how rough they've got it.''

Nancy said anxiously, ''But we don't want to break

up their friendship. That's really not our aim. We hope you understand that.''

Jenny squeezed Nancy's shoulder. "I know. And I do understand.''

"Well, then.'' Will looked grim. "Polly's in the living room.…''

The adults filed into the other room. The two girls were waiting on the couch. Amelia looked as if her world had come to an end. She had puffy, red eyes; the eyes of a girl who has cried most of the night. Polly's eyes were dry. She sat with her arms folded over her thin chest. Her strong jaw looked like granite and her mouth was a flat line. Jenny knew that look; Polly wore it too much lately—the look of the abused and misunderstood adolescent. Jenny's heart sank at the thought of the battle she faced when they got home.

She wondered, feeling exhausted and thoroughly discouraged, if there was something else she should say to the Gordons before she took her daughter and went home. She couldn't think of a thing, beyond the recriminations she longed to shout at Polly. All the classic, worried-mother things: *What were you thinking? How could you do such a thing? How can you expect me to trust you when you pull a stunt like this?*

But there was no point in going into all that now. The short conversation with the Gordons at the front door had given her what information she needed at the moment; they didn't want the girls in contact for a while, and that seemed appropriate to Jenny. The rest could wait until she and Polly were alone.

"Come on,'' she said tightly. "Let's go.''

Polly pressed her lips even harder together and

tossed her head, a gesture of pure defiance that said more than any angry words might have. The small suitcase she'd brought waited at her feet. She reached down, grabbed it and shot upright. She got about two steps in Jenny's direction when Nick spoke up for the first time since he'd greeted the Gordons at the front door. "Pol."

Polly froze. She tipped her chin higher, and pulled her shoulders back. Jenny shot Nick a look—after all, he *had* promised not to interfere.

Nick either didn't catch Jenny's warning glance, or else he ignored it. He said to Polly, "I think you owe the Gordons an apology."

Polly tossed her head again. She sucked in a breath through her nose, shuddering delicately, making it patently obvious that she considered herself the injured party here.

"Pol," Nick said again, too softly.

"Oh, all right," she snapped. She turned to Will and Nancy and spoke with lofty dignity. "I am very sorry for what happened last night. I wish it hadn't happened."

Will and Nancy stood side by side. Will put his arm around his wife and smiled sadly. "So do we, Polly," he said.

"I hope you're not going to hate me forever, because of it." Polly's lower lip quivered. She really did care what the Gordons thought of her.

"We don't hate you, honey," Nancy said. "But we don't like what you and Amelia did."

"Well, I'm sorry." She sounded more truculent than remorseful. Still, Jenny felt glad that Nick had thought to make her apologize, however grudgingly she was accomplishing it.

"All right," Will said. "Your apology is accepted."

On the couch, Amelia sniffled and let out a small sob.

Polly turned to her friend and commanded defiantly, "Hey, Mellie. Cheer up."

Amelia tried to force a brave smile.

"I'll call you," Polly promised. "Later…"

Nancy and Will exchanged a look, then glanced at Jenny. Jenny experienced a coward's urge to say nothing. To let the Gordons tell the girls what the adults had agreed on in the foyer—or to let the issue go for the moment. But the Gordons had already handled more than their share of this problem.

"You won't be using the phone for a while, Polly," Jenny said. "So you won't be calling Amelia anytime soon."

Amelia looked stricken. "Oh, no…" She sobbed again.

Polly's face turned a rageful red. "Oh, great. Fine. *Thanks,* Mom."

Polly sat in the back seat for the drive home. She didn't say a word the whole way. Jenny kept wanting to turn around and shout recriminations at her, but she made herself keep silent, in order not to say things she'd later regret.

Nick kept quiet, too. About halfway there, he turned on the radio. Jenny stared out the windshield as soft music filled the car. She felt trapped. She didn't want to look at Nick and be reminded of last night. And she didn't want to turn around, either. She didn't want to meet the angry eyes of her sulky, misbehaving daughter, who was no doubt busy staring daggers at the back of her head.

When Nick turned the Cadillac onto their street and the disaster on the front lawn came into view, Polly gave a snort of pure disgust.

"God, Mother. What did you do to the car?"

Nick shot her a quelling glance. "Watch it, Pol."

Jenny said nothing. She sat facing resolutely forward, thinking, *I will not scream at my child.*

The red wagon was gone from the driveway. Nick pulled his Cadillac in there and shut off the engine. Fingers shaking in suppressed fury and frustration, Jenny fumbled in her purse. The keys weren't there.

"Here," Nick said, holding them out.

She took the keys from him, then turned and dangled them over the seat toward her daughter. "Go in the house. And go straight to your room. Now."

Polly glared. Then, with a small, angry cry, she grabbed the keys, jumped out and bolted for the front walk.

Jenny gave her a moment to get inside. Then she turned to Nick.

Nick knew what was coming. She would ask him to leave. He tried to tell himself he understood. "Just let me put your car in the garage for you before I go. I think I can get it that far. And then, tomorrow, you can call a tow truck and have it taken care of."

His thoughtfulness totally disarmed her. And really, he had been so sweet, so silently supportive over at Amelia's house—exactly as he had promised he'd be. The only time he'd opened his mouth had been to say just the right thing: that Polly should apologize.

And was that so surprising, that he'd said the right thing? That he'd been there today, just when she needed him most?

He'd always been there whenever she or Polly needed him, ever since they'd lost Andrew. Last night should never have happened. But it hadn't changed his basic commitment to her and to her daughter.

Commitment. Yes. That was the word. Exactly the word for the way he'd always been there, ready to offer aid and comfort to his friend's widow and her child.

Jenny sighed. She was getting a headache. She rubbed her temples, willing it away. "Nick?"

"Yeah?"

"Do you…want to come in for the rest of this mess?"

He looked at her for a long, too-intimate moment. Then he said softly, "You know I do." She could see in his eyes that he wanted to reach out, to touch her. But he didn't. He tried a smile. "I still think I should put the car away first, though. Otherwise, you'll have the neighbors knocking on your door, wondering what's going on."

"Okay." She smiled back at him. "I'd appreciate that."

Inside, they found the keys on the dining room table, where Polly must have tossed them. Nick scooped them up and went out through the garage.

Jenny stood at the kitchen window, watching in a kind of a numb haze as he moved his Cadillac to the curb and then strode across the lawn to her car.

He got in, started it up. Even from inside the house, she could hear the sound of metal groaning as the tree and the car came apart. Carefully he steered the damaged vehicle back into the garage. She contemplated the tire tracks on her lawn and the gouges in the mulberry tree as she heard the garage door rumble down.

He came back into the kitchen. At the sight of him, gratitude for all his kindnesses to her seemed to wash over her in a wave. She said, "I know I don't seem very grateful, but thank you. Thank you so much."

He shrugged. "You're going to need another way to get to work tomorrow."

"My mechanic can get me a rental. I'll call him first thing."

"If you want, I could—"

"Nick. I can take care of it."

He set her keys on the counter, then ran both hands back over his hair, in that characteristic gesture that never changed a thing. The sight made her heart ache. "Sure. I know you can." He leaned a hip against the kitchen counter, waiting, she knew, for her to tell him what she wanted next.

She thought, *Hold me. I want you to hold me. I want things back as they were between us. I want our friendship. Strong and solid and not threatened by memories of last night...*

She wanted the impossible.

And she would not get it. She could tell that by the look in Nick's eyes, by the agitated beating of her own traitorous heart.

The headache behind her eyes had started to pound mercilessly. She brought up a hand to rub at her forehead.

Gently Nick said, ''Headache, huh?''

''Mmm-hmm.''

''Better take a couple of aspirin, then we'll go talk to Polly.''

Chapter Fifteen

When they entered her room, Polly lay facedown on the bed, her head cradled on her folded arms. "Go away, Mother," Polly said to the bright yellow comforter. "Just leave me alone."

Jenny drew herself up. "Polly. Sit up and look at me."

Polly stayed where she was for an insolent count of five. Then, with a great show of injured reluctance, she dragged herself to a sitting position—and saw Nick standing beside Jenny, just inside the door. "Oh, come on. Nick doesn't need to be here."

Nick folded his arms over his chest and said nothing. Jenny took her cue from him. There was a long, weighty silence, then Polly muttered, "Oh, all right. Go ahead, say it. Whatever it is, just get it over with."

Jenny schooled her voice to remain level. "I want

to hear what happened last night—from the time Will Gordon dropped you off at that party until the moment when the police brought you back to their house.''

Polly picked up one of the stuffed animals that sat on her pillow—a little pink bunny, which Andrew had chosen for her Easter basket years and years go. She sat stoop shouldered, looking down at the childish toy.

''Polly,'' Jenny tried again. ''I'm waiting.''

Polly went on staring at the bunny. ''Didn't the Gordons tell you already?''

''I want to hear it from you.''

Polly's head shot up. ''Why? So you can yell at me in front of Nick?''

''No. So I can try to understand.''

''You won't understand. You *never* understand.''

''Polly, that is not true.''

''It is.''

''It is not.''

A stare-down ensued. Polly dropped her gaze first. ''There's nothing to understand.''

''Was there drinking at that party?''

''No. They had sodas and punch and that was all.''

''Good. Was that boy there when you arrived?''

''No. Brandon showed up about nine.''

''Brandon? That's the boy's name?''

''Yeah. He asked us if we wanted to go for a ride.''

''Was he obviously drunk?''

Polly looked away. ''I don't know. He seemed… maybe. I'd never met him before. Maybe he's like that all the time.''

''Like what?''

''I don't know, Mother. He slurred his words a little,

all right? He was kind of…unsteady, when he walked, you know?''

''Yes. I do know. What happened next?''

''We went. In the car with him.''

''Why? If you knew he was drunk?''

''I don't know. He asked Mellie to go and she didn't want to go without me and I didn't want to stay alone there with all those kids I didn't even know. So I went with them, all right?''

It wasn't all right, not by a long shot. Jenny said, ''Go on.''

''He—Brandon—drove kind of crazy, I guess. And a cop pulled us over. Another cop drove up while the first cop was talking to Brandon. The second cop drove us back to Mellie's house. When we got there, the Gordons called you.'' Polly sniffed in disdain. ''You weren't home. They tried your cell phone. You didn't answer it, either.''

You weren't home. Her daughter's accusations twisted across Jenny's soul. Kids, she thought. How do they always know exactly where to slip in the knife? She ordered her thoughts off the discouraging subject of her guilt and back to the real issue at hand. ''How much alcohol did you and Amelia have to drink?''

Polly gasped. ''None. There was none at the party, I told you that.''

''Apparently this Brandon had some.''

''If he did, we didn't see it. We didn't drink anything but sodas all night. Who told you we did?''

''No one.''

Polly threw the bunny down on the bed. ''But you just *assumed* we'd do something like that?''

"I assumed nothing. I'm just trying to get at the truth here."

"Oh, right. Sure you are."

"Did you know about this boy, this *Brandon,* before last night?"

Polly traced the thread pattern on the yellow comforter. "What does that have to do with anything?"

Jenny moved fully into the room, leaving Nick alone by the door. She stood over her daughter. "Polly. Look at me."

Slowly, Polly raised her head. "What?"

"You knew about that boy before last night, didn't you? Amelia told you all about him. And neither of you bothered to say a word to your parents."

Polly blinked, then drew herself up taller. "So what? So what if she did? It was her business. I can't just tell you my best friend's private business. That wouldn't be right."

"If your best friend's private business is dangerous to her—or to you—you certainly *can* tell me. You *should* tell me. And I think you know that."

"Well, how would I know if he was dangerous? I told you, I never met him until last night." Polly was tracing patterns on the comforter again.

At that moment, as she looked down at the crown of Polly's bent head, it came to Jenny what her daughter had been doing all those nights on the phone with Amelia. "Polly. You've been *counselling* Amelia about that boy, haven't you? You've been giving her a few pointers on romance, just the same as you've been doing for Nick."

Polly's head shot up again. "No. Not the same. Not

the same at all. Amelia doesn't need to learn how to be *sensitive*. She's already sensitive. She just needed—'' Polly cut herself off as she realized what she'd revealed. Her face went red with chagrin—and defensive anger. She sucked in a hard breath and accused, ''If you think I'm so bad, what about *you?* You weren't even here when they tried to call you.''

There it was again, Jenny thought. Guilt. Staring her in the face. Speaking in her daughter's voice. Before she could recover from the shame of it, Nick moved away from the door and to her side. ''Your mother isn't the problem here.'' He spoke with suppressed fury.

Jenny put a warning hand on his arm. ''Nick…''

He shook her off.

''Nick,'' she said again. ''Let me handle—''

He ran right over her. ''You're too damn easy on her, Jen. You let her get away with murder. It's time somebody got tough on her. Time somebody made her see what a selfish little idiot she really is.''

On the bed, Polly let out a wounded cry. Jenny turned from Nick to look at her daughter again.

Polly's outraged gaze darted from Nick to her mother and back to Nick. For one hideous moment, Jenny felt absolutely certain that Polly knew what had transpired at Nick's house the night before.

But then Polly jutted out her chin at Nick. ''She's the mother. She's supposed to be *here*. She's supposed to be *responsible*.''

She's only thirteen, Jenny thought in shamed relief. She doesn't have a clue about me and Nick. She's totally wrapped up in her own tragedy right now…

''Your mother *is* responsible,'' Nick said. ''And you

know she is. Since your dad died, she's dedicated her whole damn life to you.''

"She wasn't here when they called her!" Polly was shouting now. "She didn't even leave a number where they could find her!"

Nick shouted right back. "So she's human, so what? And I'll tell you what she also *wasn't*. She wasn't out joyriding with a drunk sixteen-year-old!"

Polly flinched as if he'd struck her. Then she gathered her dignity about her once more and stuck that nose she got from Andrew back up in the air. "Everyone's against me, now. Even you, Nick. Even you…" An anguished sob bubbled up. Polly gulped, as if to push it down. But then she let it loose. With another pained cry, she threw herself across the bed, facedown. Despairing sobs fill the bedroom.

Jenny rubbed her temples, easing the headache that the aspirin she'd taken had yet to tame.

Nick blew out a long breath. "Aw, Polly…" Just like a man, Jenny thought wearily. He turns to mush at the sound of a few sobs.

Jenny stopped him as he started to move toward the bed. She grasped his arm again, more firmly this time. "Let's just leave her alone for a while."

"But—"

"Please."

He looked at her for a long moment. And then he nodded. He turned for the door.

Jenny followed him, pausing only to unplug Polly's cute yellow phone and carry it out with her.

In the family room, Jenny set the phone on the coffee table. Nick stood a few feet away, his hands stuffed in his back pockets, looking contrite. "Okay, I know

I said I'd keep my big mouth shut. I'm sorry, Jen. It's just that sometimes I think you let her walk all over you and—''

Jenny put up a hand. "She did have a point. I *wasn't* here."

He gave her a long, probing look. Then he said carefully, "Polly is thirteen years old. Old enough to go to a boy-girl party. Old enough to say no to a bad situation."

He didn't understand. He didn't *want* to understand. She sighed. "I should have been here."

Anger flashed in his eyes again. "Great. You're going to blame yourself, aren't you?"

"Part of the fault *is* mine."

He swore then.

She went on, "I should have been available. But I was with you. What Polly said is true. I didn't even leave a number where I could be reached." She dropped to the easy chair in the corner and rubbed her pounding temples again. "It *was* irresponsible of me."

"Do you blame yourself for Andy, too?"

It took her a moment to register his question. Once she did, she stared at him, feeling trapped, as he closed the distance between them and stood over her.

"Do you?"

She gazed up at him, at all that strength and manliness, thinking, I'm too tired for this now. I can't face this now. "No. Of course I don't blame myself for that. It was…an accident of fate, with Andrew. I know that. He just happened to be at the wrong place at the wrong time."

"Like Polly was last night?"

"No. It's not the same. Polly made a choice last night—"

"Right. Polly made a choice. And that choice had nothing to do with whether you were here, sitting by the phone, or not. You couldn't have kept her from making that choice, even if you sat by the phone every night of your life."

She knew he was right. Damn him. "Nick…"

"I know that tone. I know that look. You want me to stop with all these questions you don't want to answer. You want me to go."

"I…"

"It's all right. I'm going." But he didn't move.

She looked up at him in mute appeal—for what, she couldn't have said.

He put down his hand. Half reluctantly, she took it.

And he pulled her up into his arms, into his warmth and strength, into that special scent of his, and close to the deep, steady beating of his heart. He whispered against her hair, "Last night was not a mistake."

She sighed, pretended not to hear, snuggled closer, though she knew she shouldn't.

He whispered some more. "I know what you want, Jen. What you *think* you want. You and me. Like it used to be. Just friends."

She nodded against his heart, sighed once more.

"You can't have that, Jen."

She shut her eyes tight, against his too-truthful whisper, against the moment—so soon now—when he would set her away from him and walk out the door.

He took her chin, guided it up.

And then his mouth was on hers.

It was last night all over again. And everything else

went away. Nothing mattered, but his arms around her, his lips pressed to hers. She gave a cry and slid her arms up, around his neck, to pull him closer.

It lasted forever, that kiss.

Yet only for a moment.

Then he was peeling her arms away, stepping back. "I guess I've had enough training. You can tell Polly that."

She closed her eyes and pressed her lips together to keep them from quivering.

He touched the side of her face, a caress that made her skin burn and her heart beat too fast. "Open your eyes."

She did as he bade her.

"So now," he said. "You don't have to call me tonight, after all. We don't have to talk about what to say to Polly. You already know."

She swallowed. "Yes. I know."

"So are you ever gonna call me, Jen?"

She started to answer, though she had no idea what words would come out. He stopped them—whatever they were—with a finger to her lips. "Tell you what. Don't call me. Not as a friend, okay?" He bent close, brushed a kiss across her mouth. Her body yearned toward him of its own accord. But he took her by the shoulders, refused to let her cling. "Don't call me at all. Not unless you're calling as a woman to a man."

Chapter Sixteen

Jenny plodded grimly through the rest of that Sunday. Polly stayed in her room. Jenny constantly resisted the urge to go to her. She hated to admit it, but Nick had been right: Polly misbehaved too often and Jenny allowed her to get away with it. The time had finally come for Jenny to step back a little, to allow her daughter to suffer the consequences of her actions without moving right in to work things out. A day in her room was not going to kill Polly. And she just might do a little thinking about the dangerous choice she'd made at that party.

Yes, letting her stew a while was the best thing.

Unfortunately the process drove Jenny crazy.

She took two more aspirin, which finally banished her headache, and she tried to keep busy. She worked outside in the yard for a while, hacking at the ivy that constantly threatened to take over everything—and trying not to get upset about the deep gouges on the front lawn. They would grow over, she told herself. And maybe, next week, she'd get a few bags of soil and fill them in a little. New grass would grow over the gaps. By summer, no one would even know they'd been there. Of course, the mulberry tree would always bear the scars of its encounter with the back of her car.

Which reminded her. She had to deal with her car tomorrow.

So many things to deal with. The ivy, the lawn. Her car. Polly. The loss of Nick...

But better not to dwell on that right now.

It was after two when she went back inside. Polly's door, at the end of the hall, remained shut. Jenny forced herself not to go near it. She went into her own room and took a long, hot shower.

As she soaped and rinsed her body, unbidden memories rose up—of Nick's hands caressing her, of the two of them, pressed so close together on his big bed.

Hot sex.

Well, she *had* wondered what it would be like with Nick.

Now she knew.

And she feared she would never be able to forget.

Baking, she decided when her shower was done. Time to bake a few brownies. She whipped up two batches, much more than she and Polly would ever eat. But the delicious smell they made filled the house. Jenny loved that smell. It soothed her. Besides, she could take some to share at school. She'd leave them on the big table in the teachers' lounge first thing tomorrow morning and they would be gone by noon.

As she worked, she kept expecting to hear Polly's bedroom door slam. But the sound never came.

A physical ache, Jenny thought. That was what it felt like—her longing to make things right with her child. But she knew she couldn't make things right on her own. She had to have help. From Polly—who still refused to come out of her room. Polly, who should be stomping up and down the hall, banging doors, leaving her books and her papers strewn all over the table, so that Jenny would have to remind her to put them away...

It occurred to Jenny as she cut up the brownies and arranged them on twin platters, as she carefully covered them with plastic wrap, that she'd never felt so lonely since those first few months after Andrew had died.

In an effort to allay that loneliness, she called her mother and told her what had happened with Polly, carefully skirting the question of where she herself had been when the Gordons called. Kirsten listened and sympathized and reminded her that kids did make mistakes. Kirsten said that Jenny was wise, to let Polly alone for a while, to let her ponder the seriousness of what she had done.

Jenny felt a little better when she hung up the phone.

But not *that* much better.

She cooked a nice dinner: pork chops in mushroom sauce, with rice and salad and green beans. She ate her share alone, then put the rest in the fridge, thinking that if Polly came out, she could heat it up for her.

But Polly didn't come out.

Bedtime brought a sigh of relief. At least the bleak day was over. But then Jenny couldn't sleep.

At midnight, she pulled on her robe and went out to the kitchen, where she made cocoa the old-fashioned way, on the stove, in the double-boiler. She carried a mug of it into the spare room and sat down at her desk. She had a few papers she could correct, some lesson plans to go over.

But she didn't get them out. Instead she just sat there, with the chocolate-scented steam drifting up from her cup, wondering how her life could have become such a total disaster in the space of twenty-four hours.

"Mom. You made cocoa."

The small, sheepish voice came from the doorway behind her.

Jenny sat very still as tears filled her eyes. Cocoa had done it, she thought, at the same time admitting that she'd made the hot chocolate as something of a lure, just like the brownies earlier, a message in scent to her child: Here's chocolate. I love you. Jenny blinked, swallowed the tears, thinking that for once, Polly had actually managed to leave her room without slamming the door.

She turned to face her daughter, who had puffy eyes and rumpled hair and was still wearing her jeans and her wrinkled T-shirt.

"Could I have a cup?"

"Yes, you could."

Polly shifted from one stocking foot to the other. "Oh, Mom…"

Jenny stood and held out her arms. Eighty-five pounds of contrite adolescent came flying at her. Polly landed, hard, against her chest.

"Oh, Mom. Mom…" Polly pressed herself close

and burst into sobs. "I'm just a nothing. I know it. What I did was wrong. I know it was wrong. But…I didn't know what else to do. I guess I should have called Mellie's parents, or something. But that seemed so disloyal. So I…got in the car with them…."

Jenny stroked Polly's tangled brown hair. "Shh. Don't cry, now. You are not a nothing and you don't have to cry—"

"But I am. I am. The kids at school call me the Beanpole With a Brain. And Brace Face. And Jaws—"

"Oh, honey—"

"I'm just ugly, Mom. I know it. Sometimes I think…I'm getting breasts. But I'm not. I'm just kidding myself. I'm skinny and I'm ugly and no boy is ever going to like me—"

"That's not true—"

"It is—"

"Oh, honey—"

Polly pulled back and swiped at her red, runny nose. "Oh, Mom. I've been thinking. Just sitting there, all day and all night in my room, thinking. That I've been trying to help Mellie and Nick because I can't help myself. Because I'm just hopeless. And being hopeless makes me mean. So I'm a mean, ugly, brainy, skinny person—with braces. That's what I am."

Jenny put her hands on Polly's thin shoulders. She looked into those streaming green eyes and wanted to say a hundred things at once: I was skinny, too, when I was your age. And I got breasts, eventually. You will, too. Wait and see. And you are not mean. And I will kill every child who ever said a cruel word to you.

But Jenny said none of those things. She thought of

her own mother, a few nights ago. Sitting there with
her decaf, listening. Not saying all the true things she
could have said that Jenny already knew. Just showing
Jenny her love with attention, with understanding.
With the touch of her hand across the tabletop.

Polly sniffled and swiped at her nose again.

Jenny went to her desk and got a tissue from the
box there. She gave it to Polly.

"Thanks." Polly blew her nose and dabbed at her
eyes.

"Let's get you some cocoa."

"Okay."

They sat at the dining-room table together, their
cups of hot chocolate in front of them. Polly said she
did know that her braces would come off in a year or
so. That she would eventually grow breasts.

"But it's not so easy, waiting, you know? Not so
easy looking in the mirror every day and seeing a
skinny geek with a mouthful of metal."

Jenny just could not let that one pass. "You are not
a geek."

"Mom. Geek is just another word for smart person.
I am a very smart person. So, the fact is, I am a geek.
I will always be a geek—barring brain damage. Even
when I get rid of all the metal, even if I end up a
gorgeous 36C. That's my dream, actually. To be gorgeous someday. To be a gorgeous geek and a poet."

She agreed that she'd stay away from Amelia for a
while. "And I'll stop trying to help people with their
love lives. I guess I didn't do such a hot job with that,
anyway. It turned out I was helping Mellie get together
with a delinquent. And look at Nick. Is he back to-

gether with Sasha? Not. He won't even *call* her. I mean, what's the point of being in love with someone, when you won't even *try* to get them to talk to you?''

Jenny sipped her cocoa, thinking that she was going to have to say something to Polly, about Nick. She wouldn't go into particulars, of course, but she did need to explain the situation in a general way.

Not right now, though. The whole thing was just too fresh right now.

Polly had come to more conclusions, during the long hours in her room. ''And I'm willing to be grounded. I *deserve* to be grounded, I know that. I do. For…a month?''

''A month will be acceptable.''

That brought a deep sigh. ''Okay. But can I still do my tutoring on Thursdays? Those kids really need my help, you know?''

''You may do your tutoring.''

''Thanks. And I also think Nick was right in the terrible things he said to me. I mean, whatever you were doing last night that made it so you weren't here when the Gordons called, that's your business. Because, you know, I think it would be good for you, if you got a life.''

''Honey,'' Jenny said gently. ''I do have a life.''

''I know. But a *love* life. You're not *that* old, Mom. And you're pretty good-looking.''

''Why, thank you.''

''Don't thank me. It gives me hope, is what it does. Because you're my mother. I've got your genes. Maybe someday, I'll be good-looking, too.''

''You will. I promise you.''

Polly scrunched up her nose. "That's the kind of promise only a person's mother would make."

"Believe it."

"I'm trying. But everybody says I resemble Dad more than you. And he wouldn't have looked so gorgeous, as a girl."

"He was a very handsome man, your father."

"Yeah, I know. But I don't want to be *handsome*."

"*You* will be gorgeous."

"Stop it, Mom. Next you'll be telling me I'm *already* gorgeous. And then I won't be able to believe anything you say." Polly grinned then, showing metal—a very good sign.

In the morning, both Jenny and Polly woke late. They rushed around the house, Polly hurrying to make the bus, Jenny packing lunches and gulping down cold cereal between calls to a fellow teacher, who would give her ride, and to Triple-A, which would send a tow truck for her damaged car, and to her mechanic, who promised to bring over a rental car and leave it in the driveway sometime that afternoon.

When everything was arranged, Jenny went out and managed to get the car out onto the curb, where the tow truck driver would have no difficulty finding it. She put the key under the back seat mat, as she'd told the people at Triple-A she would do.

When she came back in, Polly demanded, "What *did* you do to the car, Mom? Really?"

And Jenny explained about the red wagon in the driveway and how she'd swerved to avoid it and ended up barreling across the lawn, into the mulberry tree.

"Because you were upset, about me, huh?" Polly looked sweetly remorseful.

Jenny thought, *And eaten up with guilt because I wasn't here the night before.* But all she said was, "I should have been more careful."

Polly gave her a big hug, then grabbed her pack and her sack lunch and ran out to catch the bus, slamming the door good and hard behind her.

At school that day, Jenny came into the teachers' lounge at lunchtime and found Roger eating the last of the brownies she had set on the table in the morning. He jumped when he saw her, as if she'd caught him stealing. But then he composed himself. "These are great, Jenny."

"Thanks." She smiled at him, thinking for about the hundredth time what a nice man he was, and admitting to herself that she wouldn't be going out with him again.

Roger started backing away from her. "Uh, gotta go. Gotta get back to my classroom, you know?"

She watched him go out the door, wondering vaguely if he was all right, but mostly thinking of Nick, of how she didn't want to go out with *anyone* except Nick. And going out with Nick was too dangerous, because it made her want to take certain chances she hadn't taken since she'd given her heart to Andrew Brown, at the age of sixteen. Certain chances she knew both her mother and her daughter believed she ought to take again. Chances she herself understood she probably *should* take again.

But she wouldn't. She just couldn't.

And maybe, in the end, she could have Nick's

friendship back. She couldn't help hoping that they'd both get over this whole thing. They'd put all this craziness behind them and go back to the way things used to be.

Yes, that was sure to happen. No matter what Nick had said on Sunday, he would get over her eventually. And she would get over him. All they needed was a little time…

On Wednesday night, during dinner, Polly asked, "Mom, do you think Nick's still mad at me?"

Jenny's pulse started pounding at the mention of Nick's name. She carefully swallowed before protesting, "Oh, no. Honey, I'm sure he's not."

"Well, has he called? Has he asked about me?"

"Uh, no. He hasn't called."

Polly speared a bite of roast chicken, brought it to her mouth, then set her fork down on her plate. "Well, Mom. I know I'm not supposed to help him out anymore with his love life, so I understand why he didn't show up Monday. But it's strange he hasn't even called. I mean, we've been friends since I was *born*. The only thing I can figure out is that he must be mad at me."

This is the time, Jenny thought miserably. I'm going to have to tell her *something* about Nick. But all she said was, "No. Really. I'm sure he's not mad at you."

"Well then, even though I'm not supposed to use the phone—could I, this one time, to call *him?*"

"Oh, no, don't do that!" The words just popped out of her mouth, anxious and frantic and not at all what she should have said.

Polly frowned. "Mom. This is a special situation. You know it is."

Jenny set her own fork down. What was the matter with her? Polly had her own relationship with Nick. A very important, very special relationship. The last thing Jenny wanted was to come between them.

"Mom?" Polly tried again, "Come on."

Jenny closed her eyes, took in a breath and let it out in a quick burst as she faced her daughter once more. "I'm sorry I said that. Of course you should call him."

"Mom." Polly looked at her suspiciously. "What is going on?"

Jenny blew out another gusty breath. "Oh, Lord."

Polly shoved her plate aside and leaned both elbows on the table. "You can tell me. I can handle it—whatever it is."

"Well, honey…" She lost her nerve. But Polly was looking at her, worry pinching her face. Jenny made herself say it. "Nick has decided that he needs a little time away from me."

Polly blinked. "From *you?*"

"Yes."

"But why? What did you *do* to him?"

"Um, well." Jenny pushed her own plate away. "That's a good question."

"So answer it."

"I'm trying."

They sat in silence for a moment, each staring at her unfinished meal. Jenny found she admired her daughter's patience. It was a quality she'd never seen Polly exhibit before. Finally she said, "You see, Polly. Nick wants—well, he wants more than friendship from me."

Polly's mouth dropped open. The sight would have been comical if Jenny had been in a laughing mood. "Wait a minute. You mean he wants to be your *boyfriend?*"

"Uh, yes. That's exactly what I mean."

"But what about Sasha?"

"Sasha didn't turn out to be as important as Nick thought she was."

Polly gasped, then. "Wait a minute. You were with *Nick,* weren't you? Last Saturday night?"

The best Jenny could do right then was nod.

Polly's eyes looked too big for her face. "Well. Did you…have a good time?"

"I…yes. I had a good time." A total understatement, but appropriate, Jenny thought, given the circumstances. She certainly had no intention of telling her thirteen-year-old daughter the steamy details of her torrid night with Nick.

Polly was shaking her head. "Poor Nick."

"Excuse me?"

"Well, Mom. We all know how you are."

"We do?"

Polly nodded. "You're afraid. Because we lost Dad. You won't get past the friend thing."

"The *friend* thing."

"Mom. You know what I'm talking about."

Jenny did. Too well. With some shame, she found herself wishing her daughter wasn't quite so bright.

"You've broken Nick's heart, haven't you?"

Jenny looked at her half-eaten dinner, since she didn't have the nerve to face Polly's accusing eyes. "I wouldn't put it that strongly."

''That's why he hasn't called. He's staying away from you, because you won't love him back.''

Jenny did look up then. ''Wait a minute. I did not say that word. Love was not mentioned.''

''Love doesn't *have* to be mentioned, Mother.''

''Polly. I don't like your tone.''

Polly pushed back her chair and stood. ''I'm calling him.''

The word *no* rose to Jenny's lips again. She held it back and looked pointedly up at her daughter. ''Don't try any more matchmaking. I warn you.''

Polly held her head high. ''You don't have to worry. I've learned my lesson about that.''

''I sincerely hope so.''

''But I won't stop being Nick's friend just because you're afraid to love him.''

Jenny spoke more gently then. ''Of course you won't.''

Polly's haughty expression softened, too. ''Oh, Mom. Look. I won't say a thing, about what you told me. Not unless he brings it up, okay?''

She knew Nick well enough to safely be able to say, ''He's not going to bring it up, honey.''

''Well, fine. But I do have to call him.''

Jenny made herself smile. ''I know you do. Go ahead. You can use the phone on my desk in the spare room.''

When the phone rang, Nick was sitting on the sofa, channel-surfing, with the fuzz ball in his lap. He picked up the extension on the table by his elbow.

''Nick? It's me, Polly.''

The sound of her voice reminded him of Jen. That

hurt. But he smiled, anyway. He'd been missing Polly, too. He punched the Power button and the TV screen went dark. "Hey. How are you?"

"Oh, all right. I guess. I got grounded for a month. And I'm not supposed to use the phone. But Mom said I could, this once, to call you."

Just like Jen, he thought. Making sure I don't lose Polly, too. "Well, good."

"Nick? I want you to know, I'm sorry. For being such a jerk last Sunday."

"What? A jerk? *You?*"

"Oh, stop it. I'm sorry. I am."

"Your apology is accepted."

"So...you're not mad at me?"

"Nope. Not mad at all. I was mad on Sunday, but not for long. Who could stay mad at you for long?"

"Oh, right. I'm so wonderful."

"You are. You're terrific. Even if you have zero appreciation for the greats in the NBA."

"I miss...having you come over. But I promised Mom. No more training sessions, you know?"

"I understand."

A silence. He had the distinct impression she was choosing her next words carefully, which made him wonder just what Jen had told her. "Uh, how's Daisy?"

"She's fine. She's right here. Purring up a storm."

"Have you taken her in for her shots yet?"

"Not yet."

He knew the instructions were coming. And they were. "Nick, you have to get her to the vet. And are you going to let her have a litter?"

"Litter. She's got litter. It's all over the laundry room floor."

"Nick. You know what I mean."

"Yeah. Kittens."

"Well, are you?"

"I think I'll pass on that."

"Then she has to be spayed."

He looked down at the fuzz ball. She looked up at him and purred even louder. "Gotcha." He felt like a traitor, talking about spaying right in front of her when she trusted him so much.

"Nick. I mean it. You have to get her to the vet. Those shots are *important.*"

"Okay, okay. I'll get her to the vet."

"Tomorrow?"

"I don't know, Pol. I—"

"Come on, Nick. Promise me."

"All right, all right. I'll deal with it. Tomorrow. So tell me. Read any good love sonnets lately?"

She laughed. "You know I can't talk about love sonnets with you anymore."

"Then tell me about school. Tell me about how you're getting straight *A*'s."

"Nick. Maybe we could go to a basketball game again, after I get off restriction. How would that be?"

"Wait a minute. Is there something wrong with this phone? I thought you just said—"

"You know what I said. Can we do that?"

He knew for sure then that Jen had told Polly the bare facts, at least. He didn't know how he knew—he just did. He didn't much like knowing that.

"Nick, could we do that?" She was telling him *she*

still wanted him around, even if her mother wanted nothing to do with him.

Anger moved through him. Kind of a slow burn. He kept thinking of Saturday night, kept thinking that Jen was the woman he wanted.

And she wanted him, too. Saturday night more than proved that. Still, she'd allow a dead man and her own fears to keep them both from getting what they wanted.

"Nick. Can we?"

Polly had said she was grounded for a month. In a month, it would be playoffs time. He'd have to hunt around for tickets, to an L.A. game or maybe Salt Lake City. They'd have to fly there. Probably stay overnight. And what the hell would Jen say to that?

"Nick? Are you still there?"

"Yeah, Pol. I'm still here."

"Then tell me, will you do that? Will you take me to a basketball game when I get off restriction?"

He could learn to hate Jen, he realized. He'd have to guard against that.

"Nick? Please?" She sounded so pitiful.

"Look, Pol. We'll see, okay?"

A long silence on the line. Then she said in a small voice, "Yeah. I guess so. Okay…"

Polly stayed in the spare room for fifteen minutes. When she came out, Jenny had already finished her dinner and carried her plate to the sink.

Polly picked up her own plate and brought it into the kitchen. "I've had all I want, I think." She scraped the food into the garbage and joined Jenny at the sink. Jenny took the plate from her, rinsed it and put it in the dishwasher. She'd been telling herself the whole time Polly was on the phone that she would not ask what Polly and Nick had talked about.

Polly picked up the sponge and began wiping down the counters. She glanced up, and saw Jenny watching her. "He's fine," she said.

"Good."

"He's not mad at me."

"I didn't think he was."

"I got him to promise to take Daisy to the vet for her shots and stuff."

"That's good."

Polly rinsed the sponge and wrung the water from it. She glanced at the dishwasher, at the few pots, already drying on the drainer by the sink. "You cleaned everything up already."

Jenny nodded. No reason to explain that she'd been nervous, that she'd wanted something to do while her daughter talked on the phone to the man she herself couldn't stop thinking about.

Polly dried her hands. "Well. I've got homework."

"Better get to it then."

Polly hung the towel back on its hook. "Mom. I didn't say a word about what you told me. He didn't say anything, either."

Not knowing what else to do, Jenny smiled and nodded.

Her daughter turned and disappeared down the hall.

The next morning, Roger Bayliss caught Jenny just as she was getting out of her car. "Jenny, I've been hoping to get a moment alone with you."

Jenny shut her car door and tried not to show the apprehension she felt. She just did not want to have to tell Roger that she'd changed her mind about going out with him again. He'd hardly talked to her all week, other than the brief incident with the brownies on Monday. She'd actually let herself imagine that if she kept a low profile around him, the subject might never come up.

He was carrying a big lesson plan notebook. He clutched it to his chest. "Jenny," he said grimly, "you're a lovely woman. And I never meant to lead you on..."

A cool wind was blowing. Jenny wrapped her sweater closer around herself and leaned against the door of her car, as Roger went on to explain that he and his ex-wife, Sally, were getting back together again. They'd run into each other in the supermarket Saturday and just started talking. They hadn't been apart, except to go to work, since then. Sally had finally realized that she'd let her mother come between them, and she swore it wouldn't happen again.

"I'm not expecting miracles, you know," Roger said. "But we're trying. We're working on it."

Jenny told him she was happy for him and swore she didn't feel he'd led her on at all. They walked into the building together, Roger rambling on about Sally and how wonderful it was to be working things out with her.

Jenny listened and smiled. This was perfect. Roger had his wife back—and Jenny never even had to tell him that their first date had been their last.

If only things between her and Nick could be so simple.

Since it was Polly's tutoring day, Jenny had time to stop in at Wal-Mart on her way home. She bought two sixty-pound bags of potting soil. One of the clerks helped her load it into the trunk of the rental car.

At home, Jenny parked at the curb, under the now-leafy branches of the mulberry tree. She went inside and changed into old jeans and a sweatshirt with the sleeves torn off. Then she went back out again to haul the bags from the trunk. She dragged them up on the lawn and ripped the end of one open.

She was spreading dirt into the deepest of the tire tracks when Nick's Cadillac swung into her driveway.

Chapter Seventeen

Nick got out of the car, shutting the door hard behind him. He had Daisy tucked under one arm. Jenny held on to her shovel as if it could save her from those dark eyes that seemed to stare right down into the center of her.

"We've got to talk," he said.

She swallowed convulsively, thinking, *You're not supposed to do this. You said I should call you.*

He demanded, "You want to talk here? On your front lawn?"

She let the shovel fall, then pulled off her gloves and dropped them on the ground, too. "No. Let's go inside."

He followed behind her, up to the porch, where she stomped her feet on the mat, to shake off the loose dirt. Then she went in the front door.

"Where's Polly?" he asked, when the door was shut behind them.

"It's her tutoring day."

"Good. I wanted to talk to you alone." He was glaring at her. The little cat hung under his arm, purring and completely relaxed.

The small foyer seemed way too cramped for the two of them. Jenny gestured toward the main part of the house. "Well. Come in, then."

He went ahead of her, through the dining room and down the steps to the family room. She detoured to the kitchen. "Go ahead. Have a seat. I want to wash my hands."

"Fine."

In the kitchen, she turned on the water and squirted soap on her hands. As she rubbed them together under the faucet, she told herself to relax, that whatever he was here about, she could handle it.

Too quickly, her hands were clean. She wiped them on the towel and hung it carefully back on its hook. Then she had no choice but to go to him, out through the dining room, down those two steps. He stood by the brick fireplace at the far end of the room, waiting. Not smiling. Not smiling at all…

They regarded each other down the length of the room. The little cat still hung there, under his big arm. Jenny resisted the urge to wring her hands in distress.

"What?" she said finally. "What is it? What's wrong?"

He let out a short bark of laughter. "What's *wrong?*" He started walking toward her, slowly. She had to force herself not to move, not to back away as he came near.

When he stood about two feet from her, close enough that she could have fallen right into the darkness of his eyes, he stopped. And he held out the cat.

Automatically she took the purring animal from his arms. The kitten snuggled right against her, dipping her head, inviting strokes. Jenny petted her. The soft, furry warmth felt reassuring, comforting. And with Nick so close—close enough that the scent of him taunted her—Jenny needed reassuring. She looked down at the cat, in part as a way to avoid those dark eyes. The cat stared up at her, seeming to smile.

"Take a good look." Nick growled the words. "A good, long look."

Jenny jerked her head up. "Nick. What is the matter with you?"

"Well, Jen. I'm mad. I'm steamed, as a matter of fact."

She gulped. Hard. The word *why* came into her head, but she didn't have the courage to say it right then.

"Daisy and I just got back from the vet," he said very quietly.

She gulped again. "Uh, yes. Polly mentioned that you said you would take her."

"Yeah." He loomed closer. "You know what the vet told me?"

Daisy started to squirm. Jenny realized she was holding her too tightly, an instinctive physical reaction to her own internal turmoil. She knelt and let the cat down. Daisy promptly strutted up the steps and across the dining area floor, stopping beneath the table, where she sat. Wrapping her tail around her front paws, she watched them through slitted eyes.

''You know what the vet said?'' Nick challenged again.

Jenny turned to him. ''No. But I assume eventually you'll get around to telling me.''

''Oh, I'll tell you. I'll tell you, all right. The vet laughed, that's what. He examined that cat, and then he laughed.'' He loomed even closer. ''Do you want to know why?''

She held her head high. ''Yes. I certainly do. And right away, if you don't mind.''

''Because Daisy is a *boy*.''

She stared at him, not certain she'd heard right. ''But…I checked, and so did Polly.''

''Well, you didn't check close enough—or else you damn well didn't know what to look for.''

She angled her chin higher. ''I beg your pardon. I knew what to look for.''

He let out a harsh bark of laughter. ''You knew what to look for. Sure. Sure, you did.'' He pointed an accusing finger. ''You. You and Polly. So damn sure that cat was a female. So damn sure that cat was meant for me. But did I get to name the poor guy? Hell, no. Daisy, Polly says. That cat has to be called Daisy. So now, what?''

He paused, but not long enough for her to say anything. Right away, he was barreling on. ''I'll tell you what. *She* is a *he* and the poor guy knows his name. He answers to Daisy. I can't call him Rex or Jake or some other decent guy's name. He's Daisy. Daisy. For the rest of his damn life. All because, you and Polly, you two know everything.'' He turned and paced the length of the room. When he got back to the fireplace, he faced her again. ''So now I've got a boy cat I've gotta call Daisy. And that's not all. Not only does he have a damn dumb girl's name, next week, the vet is going to cut off his—''

She put up a hand. "Never mind. I understand."

He started coming toward her again. "No, you don't. You don't understand at all. The point is, not everyone's what you want them to be, what you think they should be. Not everyone's *sensitive* and *caring*. Not everyone's willing to just be your *friend*. Sometimes, a guy is just a guy, and that's all he is. Sometimes, a guy screws up and puts the lovemaking before the talking. Sometimes he might show up at your house when he's got no business being there." He stopped a few feet from her and demanded, "Which reminds me, what the hell was going on Friday night?"

She just stared at him, wishing he wasn't so handsome, wishing he'd grab her and kiss her, wishing he'd get out and leave her alone.

He prompted, "Friday night a tall, thin guy with brown hair brought you home."

"Roger?"

"You're dating some guy named Roger?"

"No. I'm not. It was one date."

"One date?" he sneered.

"Yes. And now he's gone back to his wife."

"He's got a *wife?* You're going out with some guy with a wife?"

"No, they're divorced. Or they were, as of last Friday night. Then, a few days ago, they decided to get back together."

He looked somewhat mollified. "Well. Good for them."

"Nick. Were you *spying* on me Friday night?"

"No." He threw up both hands. "Yeah. Hell, was I? I guess. I went to the Nine-Seventeen Club and finally figured out that I didn't want Sasha. I wanted to talk to you, to tell you…hell, I wanted to see you, all right? I came here and I parked down the street and just sat there in the car, trying to get up the damn nerve to knock on your door, since you'd kicked me out the night before and told me I couldn't come back until Monday. While I was sitting there, I saw you come home, you and this Roger guy." He started to pace again, back and forth in front of her. "Yeah, all right. I know, I shouldn't have been there, since you had told me to stay away. And then later, on Saturday, before we made love, I should have told you I saw you with Roger and I should have told you about Sasha. But I didn't."

"That's what I'm telling you. That's how I am. Just a guy. I'm not the best guy. I'm not Andy, not by a long shot. Polly was wasting her time, trying to train me to be a better man. Because I'm just…who I am. Just Nick. Just a guy." He stopped, faced her again. Now, he looked at her hopelessly. "Hell. What am I doing here? I'm not here because of poor Daisy, who doesn't even know he's a boy. I'm damn mad over Daisy, but that's only an excuse to come here, to step over the line I drew myself, when I told you I wouldn't come here, that you would have to come to me. But you're not going to come to me, are you, Jen?"

He waited, standing there, so big and solid and heartbreakingly alive. The man who had hated her once, then tolerated her, then become her best friend.

The man who now wanted more from her than she could let herself give.

He said, "You think I don't know you, don't know how you are? Don't know what you're doing now, don't know how your mind works? How you're thinking that maybe, in time, I'll get over you? How things will go back to being like they were?"

He took two steps, which brought him right up to her. And then he put his big hands on her shoulders. She wanted to cry out when he touched her, cry out in longing. In hunger. In need. But she didn't do that. She made no sound at all.

"We can't go back, Jen. That's what happened on Saturday night. I took you to bed instead of saying all the things I should have said. And now we can never go back."

She refused to believe such a thing. She shook her head. "Oh, don't say that. Eventually you'll get over it. So will I. We'll be friends again...."

He looked down at her, his eyes full of pain, of limitless yearning. He said one word, "No."

"But—"

His fingers dug into her shoulders. "Damn you. I miss you. And I'm so mad at you. Because I know you. It's what happens with a friend. You know them. Like I knew Andy. Like I knew the first time he said your name, that from then on, I would be second for him. That you were gonna come first. I hated you for that, Jen. I'd been his friend since the damn sandbox. Like Polly and Amelia. We told each other everything. I always came first with him. And then you came along. And I wasn't first anymore."

"Oh, Nick. I know."

His eyes seemed to burn her. "If you know, then stop lying to yourself. We can't go back. Stop saying we can. We were enemies and then we were friends. And now, you know what's happened, Jen. Now I love—"

She couldn't bear for him to say it. She raised a hand, put it on his mouth. "Don't."

He whispered the truth at her, "You're a damn coward, Jen." His breath was warm against her fingers. And then he was pushing her fingers away. "You love me, too, Jen. I know you do."

She tried to say *no,* but the word wouldn't come out.

He said, "I want to believe that love is going to be stronger than how scared you are. All those books and poems Polly made me read say it is. All those movies. All those songs. Were they all lying, is that it?"

How could she answer that? How could she tell him—

He lowered his mouth to hers, so gently. His lips settled on hers like a breath. Like a prayer.

Her thoughts flew away.

There was only Nick. Only Nick and his kiss, his body against hers, his big arms around her, holding her close.

His tongue sought entry. She gave it. The kiss deepened. She sighed.

And then the front door slammed.

Nick raised his head. Jenny opened her eyes, bewildered, confused. He grasped her waist and moved back from her.

They both turned to look toward the dining room as Polly came bounding in.

She skidded to a stop at the sight of them. "Oh!" She looked from Jenny to Nick. "Well," she said. "Well. Uh, don't let me interrupt, okay? I'll just, you know, go on into my room." She backed toward the hall, then turned and ran off.

Two seconds later, they heard her door slam.

Nick let go of Jenny and took another step back. He ran both hands back over his hair. She wanted to cry as she watched him do that. Then he turned away from her. He went and stood at the glass door and looked out at her patio and the small lawn beyond it. "Polly knows, right—about Saturday night? About what I want from you?"

Jenny didn't answer immediately. He sent her a dark look. She nodded. "Yes, Polly knows."

He stared back out the window again. "She wants me to take her to a basketball game, when she's through being grounded. A playoff game. Can you believe that? Polly *asking* to go to a basketball game?"

"She...doesn't want to lose you, Nick."

"Yeah, I figured that out."

"I hope she won't lose you."

His big shoulders lifted, then fell with his sigh. "You women. You ask a damn lot." He turned around then, and looked at her for a long time. "It isn't just Andy, is it?"

She said nothing.

He knew the answer, anyway. "It was losing him, right?"

She nodded. "Oh, Nick. I just, I couldn't stand to go through that again."

"You wouldn't have to. I would never ask you to. I would stick by you, Jen. I know I've been a run-around. I know I made a damn fool of myself over Sasha, who never really meant a thing to me. But I can swear to you now, that I would—''

She couldn't bear for him to finish. ''Andrew swore, too, Nick. And I lost him. We can't know what will happen. Sometimes the truest promises get broken. And there are some people, like me, who just don't want to take the risk again.''

He gestured toward the hallway, where Polly had gone. ''What about her?'' He spoke low, for Jenny's ears alone. ''What about Polly? I'm a rotten jerk for mentioning it, but you could lose her. It's not likely, but it's possible. You don't...send her out of your life for that. You don't *penalize* her because an accident might happen, because she could get sick and die.''

''It's not the same. You know it. With Polly, I don't have a choice. She's my child. I have to take the chance.''

''Hell, Jen.'' He took a step toward her, and then stopped himself. He stuck his hands into his pockets, as if to keep them from reaching for her. ''You're gonna miss me, when I go. Maybe as bad as I'm gonna miss you.''

She wanted to deny that, but she just couldn't force out the lie.

He went on, ''You're gonna miss me because you love me. You do. I can see it in those blue eyes. I can feel it when you kiss me. You're gonna make us both suffer because of some remote possibility that you might lose me down the road. Is that logical? Does that make one damn bit of sense?''

She answered in a tiny voice. ''No, it doesn't. I

know it doesn't. Not to you. Not to anyone who hasn't gone through what I went through.''

"Damn it, Jen." He turned back to the window.

"No. No, listen." She dared to approach him, to stand beside him, to look out at the patio, the back lawn, the late-afternoon sun with him. "You want to know, then listen." She waited. He said nothing. She told him so quietly, "It's the little things that do it. The little things. The everyday things. The way you laugh. The way you put ketchup on your sandwiches. The way you run both hands back over your hair. It would be you, in the morning, at the table, eating breakfast, ready to look up and give me your smile. It would be us, in the same bed, every night. Because I would grow to need you there, to love you, there, in every part of my life. It would be that I would know, because it happened before, that some morning I could wake up and kiss you goodbye and you would leave, to get doughnuts, maybe, or just to go off to work. And you might…never come back.''

She couldn't stop herself. He was so close. She laid her head against his shoulder. He put his arm around her, though he didn't look at her. He remained, staring out at the backyard, just as she did. She leaned there, against him, against his warmth and his strength, wrapped in the special scent of him, though she shouldn't have. Oh, she shouldn't have.

She said, "Oh, Nick. You don't know. It's as if, when you love someone, you have to make big spaces inside yourself, to hold them, to hold all the little things that you are together. And then, if they leave you, if they die or they just go, there are such horrible, giant-size holes. Big, ugly gaps. In yourself. In your life. It's a kind of death, for the one left behind. A death worse than dying. Because you have to go on, with those holes in yourself.''

He squeezed her shoulder. She felt his lips brush her hair. ''It's too late, Jen,'' he whispered. ''Don't you get it? Those big spaces you talk about. They're already made. Inside you. Inside me. You send me away now, we both lose. We both have those big, ugly holes anyway.''

She closed her eyes against those words. ''It won't be as bad now as it would later on.''

He whispered in her ear, ''It's bad enough.'' And he kissed her hair once more.

Then he let go of her. He stepped back and took her hand, turned it over, so the palm was facing up. He reached behind him, into a back pocket, and pulled something out.

An envelope. Folded in half. He laid it in her open hand.

He said, ''Remember that night you caught Polly writing that love letter to Sasha for me?''

She bit her lip, made herself nod.

''I told Polly I couldn't write it myself. That love letters just weren't my style.''

The envelope felt light, in her hand. Light as air. Light as a breath—as a quick, brushing touch. ''Oh, Nick…''

''Shh. Listen. I wrote that for you. It's not much. It's just…what I feel.''

''I can't—''

''I know. You keep saying that. So I'm going. I am. But I want you to keep that.''

''Oh Nick, I—''

"Wait. Listen. You keep that. I don't want you to read it today. Or tomorrow, or the day after that. Just keep it. Put it away somewhere safe. For the day you change your mind."

"But I won't—"

"Don't say that. You already said it. A hundred times. I swear to you, Jen, I heard you. I did. And all I'm asking is for you to keep it. Keep it and don't read it. Unless you change your mind."

She started to speak again.

But he spoke first. "Do that for me. That one little thing. You can do that, can't you?"

She closed her eyes—as she closed her hand over the envelope. "All right."

"Good. Now look at me. One more time. And kiss me. One more time. And then I'll take my cat and go."

She opened her eyes. His dear face hovered above her own. And then his mouth came down, touched hers, so gently. So lightly. As light as the folded envelope in her hand.

He lifted his head. "Bye, Jen."

She could not say that word: goodbye, though she was the one sending him away.

"Tell Polly I'll call her, about that playoff game."

"Yes. I'll tell her."

A smile formed on his lips, then vanished. "I love you, Jen."

The kitten still waited, underneath the table. He went up the steps, knelt. "Daisy," he said. The kitten went right to him. He scooped up the animal, tucked it under his arm.

And then he left.

Jenny closed her eyes, so she wouldn't have to watch him go. She opened them again as she heard the front door click shut. She was left alone, with the letter she would never read clutched in her hand.

Chapter Eighteen

"Mom?" Polly peered around the corner from the hall.

Jenny looked up, put on a smile—as she slid her hand behind her and eased the envelope into the back pocket of her old jeans.

"He's gone," Polly said.

"Yes, honey. He is."

Polly stepped out, clear of the hallway. She came around the table and hovered at the top of the steps to the family room. "I saw him leave, with Daisy. I was standing in the hallway, Mom. I shouldn't have been. I have to stop doing that, I know. I have to stop sneaking around. But right now, I couldn't help myself. I snuck out of my room. And I stood in the hallway."

Jenny thought of the hard things they'd said, things she really didn't want Polly to know. "You heard what we said to each other, is that what you're telling me?"

"Well, no. You were talking so softly. I couldn't hear."

Relieved, Jenny chided, "It was between Nick and me. You know that."

"Yeah. I guess so. But won't you tell me—"

"I'll tell you this. He said he'd call you. To make arrangements for that playoff game."

Hope lightened Polly's sad expression just a little. "He did?" Jenny nodded. And Polly asked gingerly, "But what about…you and him?"

Jenny didn't know how to answer. She gave a rueful shrug.

A single tear slid down Polly's cheek. "Oh, Mom. You are making such a giant mistake. Just a huge, awful, giant mistake."

Jenny shrugged again. It seemed all she could do. Lift her shoulders, let them drop.

"Oh, Mom…." Polly came down the steps. "Mom."

Jenny reached out. Polly came into her arms with a sigh. Jenny embraced her, resting her cheek on her shining brown hair.

"This is hard," Polly said in a tight voice. "This is really, really hard."

Jenny just held on.

A little while later, Jenny and Polly went back outside together and finished spreading the soil into the tire tracks on the lawn. Then they came in and Jenny made dinner. For the most part, the meal was a silent one, though Jenny did tell her daughter that Daisy had turned out to be a boy.

Polly choked on a bite of meat loaf at the news.

When she was through coughing, she insisted, "But I checked. I was *sure*."

"So was I. But the vet says otherwise."

Polly shook her head. "Poor Daisy. Is Nick going to rename her—I mean, *him*."

"I don't think so. He says Daisy already knows his name."

Polly shook her head again, but said nothing more.

After the cleaning up had been done, Polly went to her room and Jenny spent a couple of hours at her desk.

Eventually bedtime came.

The house seemed so quiet that night. So quiet, Jenny couldn't sleep.

Morning took forever to come.

But it did come. Jenny got up and made breakfast, saw her daughter off to school, then went to work herself. That afternoon, her mechanic had the car ready. She drove over there, turned in the car she'd been driving and got her own back. It was as good as new. No one would ever guess she'd been so careless as to back it into a mulberry tree.

The weekend came. Saturday, Jenny worked in the yard again, planting a few annuals to brighten things up. Saturday night, she and Polly went over to Kirsten's for dinner. They stayed until about nine, then went home, watched a movie, went to bed.

She was fine, Jenny told herself.

Getting by just fine. Soon, in a month, or a year, she'd feel good again. About living. She'd sleep well again, at night. She'd lived through the loss of a husband, after all. She could live through this loss. This loss of her enemy who had then become her friend.

And then finally, her lover, for one forbidden, impossible, beautiful night.

Sunday, she and Polly went to church. They didn't go often enough, really. After Andrew died, Jenny couldn't bear to go. She'd felt so betrayed, by life—and by God. Slowly, in the past couple of years, she'd started going again, now and then. And it did soothe her, to sit in the pew, to sing the old hymns and listen to the minister talk about the light of the world.

She dropped Polly off at Kirsten's after the service. Kirsten had a big school project she was putting together. Polly had said she would help with it. Kirsten would bring her back home about five and share dinner with them.

At home alone, Jenny ate lunch. Then she carried the full laundry basket out to the garage, put in a load of jeans and dark shirts, poured in the detergent and started the cycle.

From the kitchen, where she stood grating cheese for a taco casserole, she could hear the washer running, humming away. She'd grated about a cup and a half of cheddar when she suddenly remembered.

Nick's letter to her.

It was still in the back pocket of her old jeans. And her old jeans were—

Jenny dropped the hunk of cheese and tossed down the grater. She flew out the garage door to the washer and flung open the lid.

Suds and drenched denim confronted her. Moaning a little, she stuck her hand in there, hooked up one pair of jeans after another, until she found the pair she sought. She dragged them out, dripping suds everywhere and felt in the back pocket.

It was there. Soaking wet, but there.

Carefully she pulled it free.

Wet through. It came apart in her hands as she tried to flatten it out.

Her hands. They were shaking. And the tears. They were falling. On her hands. On the sodden, ruined envelope, making everything wetter still.

Sobbing, she sank to her knees on the floor of the garage. With those hands that wouldn't stop shaking, she peeled the pieces of wet envelope open, revealing the drenched, torn paper inside.

She tried to smooth the two pieces on her knee. But they came apart, into four pieces. The pieces had writing on them. But it had all run together. She couldn't make out a line of it. Not a word. Nothing.

Running ink squiggles on wet paper. All she had left of Nick's message to her.

Sitting there on the cold concrete floor of her garage, Jenny rocked back and forth, moaning, tears streaming, with the ruined love letter clutched to her breast.

Forgotten. Or maybe not forgotten. Neglected. Purposely ignored. Not put away, as she had promised. Not saved, treasured, as it should have been. But stuck in the wash.

Now she would never know. What he had written. What he had said to her, what he'd wanted to tell her, if she ever got up the courage to love again.

She'd never know.

Unless she asked him.

Jenny reached up, put her hand on the washer, to give herself support. Carefully she levered herself to her feet. She set the soggy bits of paper on the dryer, put her jeans back in the washer and closed the lid.

The cycle started in again. Humming away.

Jenny gathered up the ruined bits of her letter and went back inside. She set the sodden pieces down on the counter pass-through to the living room, smoothing them out again, matching the torn edges. When it dried, she would tape it together—an exercise in futility, surely, since if she couldn't read it now, she wouldn't be able to read it when it was dry. But somehow, right then, it seemed that belated care was better than no care at all.

When the letter was neatly spread, the torn ends set back together, Jenny went to the hall bathroom to blow her nose and rinse the tears from her face. Then she returned to the kitchen and continued grating the cheese.

She'd run the hunk of cheese along the grater three times when she glanced up and saw a robin hopping across the lawn out in front, moving in and out of the shadows cast by the leaves of the mulberry tree, stopping now and then to peck the ground. As Jenny stared, the robin lifted its head and tipped it sideways, the way birds do. It seemed to Jenny that the bird was looking right at her through the kitchen window, studying her with one tiny dark eye.

Jenny set the cheese down, and the grater beside it. She rinsed her hands, dried them, then turned to pick up the phone on the wall of the pass-through. She auto-dialed Nick's number, her heart pounding so hard she could barely hear the ringing on the other end—the ringing that ended with a click and Nick's recorded voice instructing her to leave a message.

Jenny hung up the phone. "He's not there," she said to the tattered, wet bits of paper on the counter beside her. She gulped in a breath, let it out slowly, repeated, "He's not there."

She would have to try again later.

And she would. She would do it. She would keep calling until he answered in person, when she could demand, Tell me. What did you write to me? What did you say?

She turned back to her work at the other counter. She picked up the grater. Strangely, out the window, the robin remained in exactly the same position, small head tipped, looking at her.

It came to her.

Right now, there was something else.

Somewhere she had to go.

Somewhere that couldn't wait another day, another hour.

She set down the grater and left the kitchen. She needed her purse and the keys to the car.

She saw the black Cadillac, gleaming in the sun a few spaces away when she pulled into the cemetery lot. She got out of her car and stood looking at Nick's car for a long moment, wondering why she wasn't surprised.

She turned for the pebbled path, thinking of spring. Somehow, in the past few weeks, spring had crept up on her. The lawns looked so lush and green. And the trees had all their leaves. Overhead, the sky was a soft expanse of pale blue. The songs of mockers and the squawking of blue jays filled the air.

Jenny walked along the pebbled path and across the cute little redwood bridge that spanned the small creek. She saw Nick before he saw her.

At the sight of him, she stopped on the path, half in and half out of the shadow of an oak tree.

He sat on the small stone bench at the foot of Andrew's grave, leaning forward, elbows on his spread knees. He seemed to be talking. Whispering very low, though there was no one nearby to hear.

Jenny thought the word, *love.* I love him. I do. A warmth spread through her, a soft warmth, as reassuring and tender as the spring day.

Slowly Nick turned his head. He seemed no more surprised to see her standing there than she had been at the sight of his car in the parking lot. "Hi."

"Hi."

He moved over a little, making room for her. She left the half-shadow of the oak and took the place he offered.

They sat there for a time, listening to the birds singing, watching the patterns of sun and shadow through the trees. Across the sloping lawn, at another grave, a woman with white hair was arranging a bouquet of daisies in a Mason jar. When she had the flowers as she wanted them, she propped the jar by the headstone, then she stepped back, bent her white head and closed her eyes. After a moment or two, she turned toward the path and walked away in the direction of the redwood bridge.

Jenny's gaze fell on Andrew's headstone. She read, as she had read a thousand times: Husband Father Son Friend.

She turned to Nick then, her heart rising, the corners of her mouth lifting in a tentative smile. "Who were you talking to just now?"

He dipped his head, looked down at his spread knees.

"Nick, please tell me. Who were you talking to?"

"Andy." He spoke to the ground between his booted feet. "When things get bad, I come here. I talk to Andy. It makes things better, I don't know why." He dared to look up again, into her eyes. "Crazy, huh?"

She shook her head. "No. Not crazy. Not at all." She turned her gaze away from his, toward the headstone again, and confessed, "I left your letter in my jeans. Then I washed them. It's ruined. All the words ran together. I...don't know what it said."

He moved then, beside her. He took her chin, so lightly, on the tip of a finger, and guided it around so their eyes met once more. "What are you telling me?"

"I...that I want to know, what it said."

His eyes scanned her face, seeking, hoping, yearning. He let out a breath. "Nothing that you don't already know. It said I love you. It said I want you. It said you should call me. Immediately."

She took his hand, kissed it, lowered it so their two hands lay between them. "I did call you. You weren't home. Then I had this...feeling, to come here."

He didn't say anything, but he did squeeze her hand.

She squeezed back. "Love is a funny thing."

He grunted at that and spoke gruffly. "I don't think it's so damn funny."

She felt a rueful smile curve her mouth. "All right, maybe funny is the wrong word. Maybe 'miraculous' would be better."

He still wasn't buying. "What's so miraculous about it?"

"Well, it…grows. And it's always there, waiting, for us to grow, too."

He let out a low sound. "Come on, Jen. Maybe I come here and talk to a dead guy. Maybe I found out I can relate to a cat. Maybe I even managed to write a damn love letter. But I just don't get this mystical stuff."

She hid her smile and said, "I loved Andrew."

"Damn it." He tried to pull his hand from hers, but she held on. "I know you did. You don't have to rub it in."

She bumped her shoulder against his. "Nick?"

"What?" He growled the word.

"Let me finish."

"Fine. Finish."

She leaned against him. "I loved Andrew. And Andrew is dead and I thought it would kill me. But it didn't. I lived. I lived to fall in love with you, Nick."

He whispered then, "Would you say that again?"

So she did. "I love you, Nick. And it's the real thing. As real as it was with Andrew. It's…what both you and Polly have been trying to tell me. That Andrew is dead. But not really gone from us. That we are so fortunate. We knew him. He was half of what made Polly. He was a wonderful husband to me. And a true friend to you. And you and me, we…found each other, because of him. I've been such a fool, to turn away from that. To try to hide from it. To think that by turning my back on it, I could make it go away. It won't go away. Never. Not this love I feel for you. It's…just as you said, Nick. The damage is already done. The spaces are already made, in my life, in my heart. I can't make them go away by pretending they're not there."

Nick put his mouth against her ear. She shivered at the touch of his lips on her skin. "Just tell it to me straight. Are you asking me to marry you?"

She turned, enough so her mouth was almost touching his. "I want us to be a family. You, me and Polly. I'd like us to marry, you and me. And I want you to build us a house. *Our* house, the three of ours—with a little extra room in it, in case more kids come along. Do you want that?"

He said her name against her lips. And then he kissed her. It was more than answer enough.

After a moment, he pulled away and looked at her. "Yes," he said, just in case she hadn't understood before.

With a sigh, she leaned her head on his shoulder. They sat like that for a long time.

Then, in low tones, they began to plan the future they would share.

As they whispered together, a gentle breeze came up. The oak branches rustled. And a robin swooped down, perched on Andrew's headstone—and lifted its head in joyous, full-throated song.

* * * * *

**In March 1999 watch for a brand-new
book in the beloved MacGregor series:**

THE PERFECT NEIGHBOR
(SSE#1232)

by

 # 1 *New York Times* bestselling author

NORA ROBERTS

Brooding loner Preston McQuinn wants nothing more
to do with love, until his vivacious neighbor, Cybil
Campbell, barges into his secluded life—and his heart.

**Also, watch for the MacGregor stories
where it all began in the exciting 2-in-1 edition!**

Coming in April 1999:

THE MacGREGORS: Daniel—Ian

Available at your favorite retail outlet,
only from

If you enjoyed what you just read,
then we've got an offer you can't resist!

Take 2 bestselling
love stories FREE!

Plus get a FREE surprise gift!

Coming soon from bestselling
Special Edition author
Christine Rimmer

HUSBAND IN TRAINING
available March '99

Widow—and single mother—Jenny Brown reluctantly agreed to give her best buddy, dashing ladies' man Nick DeSalvo, lessons on being a sensitive husband. But before long she decided *she* wanted to play the wife....

Conveniently Yours

MARRIED BY ACCIDENT
available June '99

The Bravo Family is back—only this time, one of the Bravo *sisters* finds love where she least expects it!

Available at your favorite retail outlet.

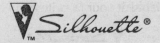

Silhouette®

Silhouette SPECIAL EDITION®

That's My Baby!

**Don't miss these poignant stories coming to
THAT'S MY BABY!—only from
Silhouette Special Edition!**

December 1998 THEIR CHILD
            by Penny Richards (SE# 1213)
Drew McShane married Kim Campion to give her baby
a name. Could their daughter unite them in love?

February 1999 BABY, OUR BABY!
            by Patricia Thayer (SE# 1225)
Her baby girl would always remind Ali Pierce of her
night of love with Jake Hawkins. Now he was back—
and proposing marriage!

April 1999 A FATHER FOR HER BABY
            by Celeste Hamilton (SE #1237)
When Jarrett McMullen located his long-lost runaway
bride, could he convince the amnesiac, expectant
mother-to-be he wanted her for always?

THAT'S MY BABY!
*Sometimes bringing up baby can bring surprises...
and showers of love.*

Available at your favorite retail outlet.

Silhouette®

Look us up on-line at: http://www.romance.net   SSETMB2

Silhouette®

SPECIAL EDITION®

COMING NEXT MONTH

#1237 A FATHER FOR HER BABY—Celeste Hamilton
That's My Baby!

When Jarrett McMullen saw Ashley Grant again, the sweet beauty he'd once loved and let go was pregnant—and alone. And though the amnesiac mother-to-be couldn't remember her past, Jarrett was determined to claim a place in her future—as the father of her child....

#1238 WRANGLER—Myrna Temte
Hearts of Wyoming

Horse wrangler Lori Jones knew she'd better steer clear of Sunshine Gap's ruggedly appealing deputy sheriff, Zack McBride, who was close to discovering her darkest secret. But then the sexy lawman took her boy under his wing—and made a lasting impression on Lori's wary heart!

#1239 BUCHANAN'S BRIDE—Pamela Toth
Buckles & Broncos

He was lost and alone...but not for long. As luck would have it, feisty cowgirl Leah Randall rescued the stranded stranger, tenderly took him in and gave him all her love. But would their blossoming romance survive the revelation that this dynamic man was a long-lost relation of her sworn enemy?

#1240 FINALLY HIS BRIDE—Christine Flynn
The Whitaker Brides

After nearly a decade, Trevor Whitaker still left Erin Gray breathless. Their bittersweet reunion brought back memories of unfulfilled passion— and broken promises. But her ardor for this devastatingly handsome man was intoxicating. Would Erin's fantasy of being a Whitaker bride finally come true?

#1241 A WEDDING FOR MAGGIE—Allison Leigh
Men of the Double-C Ranch

When Daniel Clay returned to the Double-C ranch, the tormented cowboy knew he was unworthy of his beloved Maggie. But when their night of love left Maggie pregnant, Daniel stubbornly insisted on a convenient union. But then a headstrong Maggie made a marriage demand of her own....

#1242 NOT JUST ANOTHER COWBOY—Carol Finch

Alexa Tipton had her fill of charming rodeo men. So the serious-minded single mom was beside herself when she became irresistibly attracted to the fun-loving Chance Butler. The sexy superstar cowboy began to melt her steely resistance, but could she trust their happiness would last?